Shadow Watch

LINDA CONRAD

™ MILLS & BOON®

Pure reading pleasure

*First published in Great Britain 2007
by Harlequin Mills & Boon Limited,
Eton House, 18-24 Paradise Road, Richmond, Surrey TW9 1SR*

ISBN: 978 0 263 85746 7

46-0907

*Harlequin Mills & Boon policy is to use papers that are
natural, renewable and recyclable products and made from
wood grown in sustainable forests. The logging and
manufacturing processes conform to the legal environmental
regulations of the country of origin.*

*Printed and bound in Spain
by Litografia Rosés S.A., Barcelona*

LINDA CONRAD

Award-winning author Linda Conrad was first inspired by her mother, who gave her a deep love of storytelling. "Actually, Mum told me I was the best liar she ever knew. And that's saying something for a woman with an Irish-storyteller's background," Linda says. In her past life Linda was a stockbroker and certified financial planner, but she has been writing contemporary romances for six years now. Linda's passions are her husband, her cat named Sam and finding time to read cosy mysteries and emotional love stories. She says, "Living with passion makes everything worthwhile." Visit Linda's website at www.LindaConrad.com, or write to her at PO Box 9269, Tavernier, FL 33070, USA.

With my greatest thanks to Catherine E Budd, MSN, APRN, BC, ARNP, who generously agreed to take the time to read through this manuscript when she is one of the busiest people I know. Your dedication and professionalism inspire me, Cathy, and I give you my humble thanks for all your support! Any mistakes or author-creative liberties remaining are strictly my own.

Chapter 1

"That Raven Wash kid must be drunk," someone in the crowd yelled. "He's acting crazy. Watch out!"

Dr. Victoria Sommer jumped to her feet but couldn't see a thing over the two old men with the tall black felt hats who were standing in the row below hers. They were doing the same thing she was—the same thing everyone in the auditorium was doing—trying to see to the gym floor below.

Confused by the sudden chaos, Tory shoved her way into the aisle, hoping to see what was going on. She'd been living and working on the Navajo Big Reservation for only three months, but already a few truths about her patients and colleagues had become perfectly clear.

She'd learned that traditional Navajos were conditioned to take all things in moderation—making them the most patient, the most quiet and sometimes the most infuriatingly late people she had ever encountered.

Save for a few medical emergency exceptions, no one rushed and no one shouted. So when a long-haired younger man knocked into her shoulder as he dashed down the aisle and disappeared into the disturbed crowd, Tory was shocked.

First shouting and now running? Something was very wrong.

Thinking this sudden excitement might be one of those rare medical exceptions, Tory decided she had better see for herself if this was a situation where a doctor could be of help. She wove her way through milling spectators, excusing herself as she headed down the bleacher steps toward the high school's gym floor.

Only a few moments ago the Raven Wash senior wrestling team had been about to win their quarterfinal match against the Owl Springs Boarding School team. Then something had stopped the meet.

She picked up speed as the skin on the back of her neck began to prickle, giving her goose bumps and a case of the jitters. Whatever this was had to be way out of the ordinary, and quite possibly dangerous, as well.

The real reason she'd come tonight was that there were no team doctors available for most of the high schools on the reservation. Tory had thought she would check it out, and then maybe find a way to organize a volunteer group from her clinic to fill in the gaps.

It was a rather presumptuous idea for a non-Navajo newcomer, but she'd decided to give it a shot anyway. In her professional opinion, medical practitioners and the proper medical equipment needed to be standing by at all sports meets, regardless of how far out in a poor rural area they might be.

The wrestlers at tonight's meet seemed fit enough for

competition, but she hadn't spotted any safety measures or special equipment. There should have been a portable defib machine and precautionary oxygen.

Another surge of foreboding tingled its way down to her gut. Dr. Hardeen, the chief of medical staff and founder of the Raven Wash Clinic, would not be happy if he knew she'd even attended tonight's match. When she'd first arrived to fulfill her obligation to the National Health Service, he'd warned her in the strongest terms that it was dangerous to travel alone on the reservation at night. But the high school gym was located less than a mile from the house she was renting, and she hadn't thought there would be any trouble.

Tory reached the gym floor just as a human ring began forming along the outer edges of the wrestling mat. As she pushed through the crowd, she saw a ranting Raven Wash senior wrestler pacing around the regulation twenty-eight-foot-diameter mat, while his opponent lay sprawled and unmoving in the middle. The crowd was keeping a discreet and quiet distance from the two teens.

The circling wrestler shouted something in Navajo and shook his fists in the direction of several other athletes. As far away from the disturbed kid as Tory was, it didn't take a medical degree to guess that he was high on some kind of drug. She'd seen this same violent reaction plenty of times when she'd done her E.R. rotation at Cook County Hospital.

Alcohol seemed unlikely in this case, despite what had been shouted out earlier. Liquor was outlawed on the reservation, and of course, none was allowed in the gym. This particular young man had been alert and wrestling according to the rules just moments ago, so a hallucinogenic was more likely the cause.

"What's he saying?" she asked the gray-haired woman standing on her right.

Dressed in a long-sleeved magenta blouse and a floor-length, multicolored skirt, the woman turned a sharp eye in her direction but said nothing. Tory wondered if the lady spoke any English. Another thing she'd learned since first coming to the clinic was that most people on the reservation spoke some English, but many of the elder Navajos refused to do so.

"He says he has a knife," said a male voice on her left.

Tory turned and came face to bicep with the same long-haired man who had knocked into her in the aisle. She recognized his black long-sleeved shirt and the twin bands of silver and turquoise on his wrists.

"Do you think he does?" she asked as she raised her chin to study the tall man's hawklike profile.

As far as she'd seen, the aggressive teenager who was making all the trouble couldn't possibly have a weapon on him. Not secreted in his skintight uniform, and obviously not in his empty, waving fists.

The man to her left answered the question by shaking his head, causing the ends of his long, loose hair to sway and spread across his shoulders. But he kept his eyes trained ahead on the disturbing scene.

"Not likely," he said in a low murmur. "But that doesn't mean the kid won't be dangerous. He's incoherent. And so far he's broken at least one bone in his opponent's leg with his bare hands."

That got Tory's attention. She stood up on her tiptoes and peered around the woman beside her. When the crowd shifted, she got her first clear view of the whole scene and the prone body of the other wrestler. He lay facedown and still, but one of his legs was turned askew in a most unnatural position. She'd bet even money that more than two bones were fractured in that leg.

Tory needed to get a better look. "Why doesn't someone do something?" she asked of no one in particular. "We need to get to the injured boy. I'm a doctor. I can help." She took an unthinking step toward both teens.

A hand snaked out and gripped her by the arm, keeping her firmly in place. "I am also a doctor," the same stranger to her left told her in a stilted but firm voice. "But it won't help if a bystander comes to harm while trying to intervene. The tribal police have been notified and will bring the paramedics. Wait."

"But…" She swung left, glaring up into the man's face—and immediately forgot how to talk.

It wasn't his obviously splendid physique, though it did seem perfect at a little over six feet with broad shoulders and muscles in all the right places. It wasn't his chiseled cinnamon features, either, though the strong chin and prominent cheekbones were masculinity personified in Tory's opinion.

And it wasn't even the startling and penetrating deep brown eyes that at the moment were staring into hers. It was none of those things and all of them put together that had rendered her speechless.

With implicit strength and a megawatt sensuality that probably knocked most women off their feet, the guy was not at all what Tory had expected. Her body's heightened awareness at the sight of him was also confusing.

Her palms were suddenly damp, and her brain turned to mush. She felt electrified and itchy, quite unlike anything in her experience. Which was ridiculous.

She'd grown up with four brothers. She'd been married and divorced. She'd gone to med school and interned in classes made up of fifty percent males. Nearly all her professors had been men.

She was thirty-three years old and a physician, for pity's sake. Tory simply did not grow weak and trembling at the mere sight of an…admittedly…virile man.

Just then she experienced an adrenaline rush that came hard and fast and right on the heels of the more erotic hormones already racing through her veins. She had to move. Get away. Do something.

Twisting her whole body with a sudden, jerky movement that she'd learned in martial arts class, Tory broke free of the good-looking guy's grip and stumbled onto the wrestling mat. A collective gasp ran through the crowd. Everyone seemed to be holding their breath, waiting to see what would happen next. Everyone including the bug-eyed high school senior, who stopped screaming and stood perfectly still. He stared menacingly at the strange white woman.

"It's okay," Tory told the agitated athlete in her most soothing voice. "Really. I'm a doctor." She reached out toward the drugged kid with both hands, trying a quietly pleading gesture. "Please. Let me help."

The young man took a hesitant step back. Tory figured he must be shocked by her incomprehensible movements. She was slightly taken aback by them herself.

But she couldn't afford to be afraid. Now that she was this close, she could hear the moans of the athlete who lay facedown on the mat. He was alive, but she had to stop him from trying to move.

Focusing on the semiconscious kid and trying to assess the extent of his injuries, Tory disregarded her own safety and turned her back on the crazed wrestler. With no thought to the consequences, she knelt down on the mat beside the downed teen and began checking his pupils and respiration.

Dr. Ben Wauneka didn't stop to think. If he had, he would've done a lot of things differently.

But he'd been having a major problem with his reactions to the spectacular blond stranger who'd claimed to be a doctor. He'd been doing just fine, right up until the moment she'd turned those soft, blue-gray eyes in his direction. Then all his thoughts had centered on them and on the full lips located tantalizingly below that perky little turned-up nose.

She looked like a white man's version of an angel. And he'd never wanted to kiss an angel before.

Kiss? Was he totally insane? There were so many reasons why he couldn't…shouldn't let himself feel…

A loud grunt finally tore his attention away from the angel on her knees. The drugged-out wrestler, standing about ten feet from her, seemed to have quickly gotten over the shock of the *bilagáana* woman's strange behavior. Or maybe the drugs in the teen's system simply wouldn't let him remain inert for any longer.

Whatever the reason, the wrestler roared with blind anger, fisted his hands over his head and took a few steps in her direction.

Ben's body moved without his full consent. Before he realized what he'd done, he was standing between the crazed teen and the blonde.

Using surprise in the hopes of putting the kid off balance, Ben tried a distinctly non-Navajo move and rudely stared straight into the wrestler's eyes. But instead of seeing the blank stare of a teenager strung out on drugs like he'd imagined, Ben caught a brief glimpse of something he hadn't expected to see at all.

The evil ones. Right there in this young man's eyes.

Ben was the one who'd been surprised. A second later, with momentum in his favor, the wrestler's fists came down against Ben's chest and knocked the wind out of him. Gasping for breath, Ben made a desperate move, trying to keep the kid from getting past him. He swung his arms out.

Catching the teenager by the shoulders, Ben took them both down. As he heard the sharp crack of his own forehead connecting with the hardwood floor, Ben was vaguely aware of being tangled up with a hellcat.

Before he blacked out, his thoughts went in a strange direction. Suddenly he was surrounded by warm sensations and secret sensual invitations—and all were emanating from soft blue-gray eyes.

"You should go home now, Dr. Sommer," the Navajo nurse-practitioner urged as the two of them stepped out of Dr. Ben Wauneka's semiprivate room at the Raven Wash Clinic. "You have done everything you can for him tonight."

Tory sighed and shook her head. "You're shorthanded, Russel. And with several of the beds already filled, it'll be tough finding someone to check on Dr. Wauneka through the night." She'd noticed the man's name badge said he was Russel Beyal, M.S.N., A.P.R.N., A.R.N.P., the nurse-practitioner in charge.

"Very well," Russel reluctantly agreed. "But there's a cot set up in the break room if you need it."

Taking the opportunity for a moment's rest, Tory leaned back against the corridor wall and watched as Russel turned and headed down the hall toward the nurses' station. She'd been thoroughly taken aback tonight by meeting this young male nurse, who claimed he'd been working at the clinic for several years.

She'd been working at Raven Wash Clinic herself for three months now and assumed she knew everyone involved with the place. But when she'd arrived an hour ago, right behind the ambulance bringing Ben Wauneka to the clinic for observation and treatment, Russel had greeted her at the door and told her he was in charge of clinic staff for the three-to-eleven shift.

At first sight, Russel had given her the creeps. Tory wasn't too sure why. He was wearing a white doctor's lab coat over jeans and his hair was cut short in a clean style like most of the staff. But something about his piercing black eyes bothered her. Sort of made her skin crawl.

Tory scrubbed a hand over her eyes. She hadn't taken any night shifts at the clinic since coming to the reservation because of Dr. Hardeen's caution about traveling alone after dark. And staying at home in bed for eight full hours of sleep had been a real luxury after her residency and the nutty twenty-hour shifts it had required.

Plus, there didn't appear to be much need for a physician during the dark shifts at the clinic anyway. To her knowledge, Ben Wauneka was the first patient to be checked in during non-daylight hours in the entire time she'd been here.

The door to Dr. Wauneka's room pushed open and April Henry joined her in the hall. The Navajo licensed practitioner was a familiar face for Tory. A woman in her mid-thirties, April often worked the day shift at the clinic. Tory knew her to be conscientious and a hardworking nurse.

Raven Wash Clinic had several foreign staff members. The Taiwanese surgeon, for instance, and the Mexican dentist, along with several Filipino nurses. But tonight two

Navajo nurses were on duty at the same time. Tory knew
Dr. Hardeen would rather have hired all Navajo staff, but
there simply weren't enough trained Navajo medical practitioners who were willing to come back to the reservation and work at such a small, remote clinic.

It seemed a shame. But on the other hand, it had given
Tory the opportunity to pay off her loan.

"Dr. Wauneka is finally resting," April informed her.

"That's good. I'll check on him in a minute."

"You're going to stay?"

"Someone has to wake him up periodically and check
his vitals," Tory said with a grim nod.

April's face cracked with something that nearly resembled a smile. "He *can* be rather fierce for a patient who's
only half awake, can't he? But I wouldn't mind the job. He's
a cousin, but I've always thought he was one sexy dude."

It took a huge effort for Tory to control the wry smile
that was trying to break across her own face. "You have
other patients who need you. I'll stay."

"Are you two dating?" April asked out of the blue.

Tory's sharp laugh sounded more like a hiccup. "God,
no. What would make you think so?"

"You came in with him tonight, for one thing," April
said with shrug. "I thought you didn't go out alone at
night. And for another, I'm sure he's not been in the Raven
Wash Clinic since you've come, but you seemed to know
him."

Tory thought back to the chaos at the gym. "I only
know what that tribal police officer—uh…Officer Hunter
Long, I think his name was—I only know what he told me.
He said Dr. Wauneka is a physician whose practice is centered mostly in a clinic over near Toadlena. I don't know

anything else about the doctor, except that he may have saved my life."

April raised her eyebrows at that and Tory noticed once again that the woman's long, narrow face was truly beautiful. "I heard some of what happened at the gym. Didn't know you were the crazy white… Oh, sorry. Anyway, Dr. Wauneka is born to the Big Medicine People for the Many Hogans Clan. That makes him one of my cousins, and ineligible to date.

"He is also a crystal gazer and listener," April continued. "I have a friend who went to him for a diagnosis and was pleased with the results."

"A crystal gazer. What's that?"

"Crystal gazers are traditional *Dine*…oh, that means the Navajo people, you know? Anyway, crystal gazers are medicine men. A good one can see an illness without even laying hands on the sick patient. Though I know Ben Wauneka also uses X-rays and blood tests for his diagnoses."

Tory didn't say what she was thinking. She didn't want to insult April or her beliefs. But it was absolutely incomprehensible that an educated nurse could believe such unscientific foolishness.

She decided to change the subject. "If you're three-to-eleven shift, won't you have to go home alone in the dark?"

"I'm pulling a double shift tonight so it doesn't matter. But normally my boyfriend drops me off and picks me up if I'm working after dark." April made a face. "Silly to be afraid of a natural thing like the night if you ask me. I grew up here. Darkness can be a good friend. It can heal the wounds that show up in the glaring light of day."

"So you're not afraid of Dr. Hardeen's warnings about being out alone?"

April shook her head. "It isn't just him. My boyfriend. My cousins. Most of the males in my family." She shook her head again. "Such nonsense."

"So things haven't always been that way?"

"No," April said with a frown. "A couple of years ago everybody started getting real skittery at dusk."

"What do you think happened to make them change?"

With an abrupt movement, April straightened her shoulders and raised her chin. "I have no idea. And if you'll excuse me, I have to get back to work." She turned and practically ran down the hallway, leaving Tory standing all alone.

Well, that was odd.

Ben sensed her presence even through the fog in his brain. He took a chance and pried open one eye.

Yep. It was the angel doctor, all right. Just the sight of her cornsilk blond hair pulled back in a bun on the top of her head made him feel like he might actually live.

She was checking his oxygen saturation levels and reading the blood pressure monitor. In a moment, she'd be propping open his eyelids to check the pupils and their reaction to the light.

He would save her the trouble. "Whaa…" Oh, man, was his throat dry. He tried to clear it and ended up having a coughing fit instead.

"Take it easy," she told him in that angelic voice. "Let's try a little water. That should help."

The pretty blonde lifted his head and put a cup to his lips. A couple of swallows and his throat felt better. But then he realized how nauseated and dizzy he was.

Ben clamped down on the light-headed feelings. "What's your name?" Well, that wasn't what he'd been prepared to ask. But now that he had, he thought it was certainly a terrific question.

"I'm Dr. Victoria Sommer, Dr. Wauneka. And I owe you a big thanks."

"Ben," he squeaked. He swallowed and tried again. "The name's Ben."

"Okay. Then you can call me Tory." She lifted the small flashlight and checked both his pupils.

"I assume I have a concussion and not a fractured skull. Is that your diagnosis?"

"That's my best guess, yes," she told him. "But I'm considering transferring you to the Indian Health Services facility in Gallup for an MRI just to be sure."

"I don't need it. Don't bother. Uh…where am I?" He'd known it was a clinic, but where?

"We brought you to the closest place. The Raven Wash Clinic. The young man you saved was taken to Gallup after the paramedics stabilized him and braced his neck and legs. His left femur was fractured in several places."

"What about the other wrestler? The one that took me down?"

The beautiful angel doctor shook her head sadly. "I… Sorry. I don't think he survived."

"What?" Ben hadn't thought the young man was that overdosed. In fact, he'd figured the kid had been taking steroids and could be saved with some real effort at rehab.

"The tribal cop who came had to use a stun gun on him to keep him from killing all of us." She shrugged one shoulder. "Maybe…" She left the thought unfinished.

"Did they take the body to Farmington?" Ben knew it would be against the family's wishes, but he wondered if there would have to be an autopsy. The closest place for that was the Farmington hospital.

"I'm not sure. But the policeman said he would stop in to talk to you about it tomorrow."

He relaxed back against his pillows. Remembering through the haze of pain that the cop had been Hunter Long, Ben knew he would bring answers. Hunter was in the Brotherhood. Ben trusted him completely.

"Can you get a little rest now?" the angel asked in that easy, melodic tone of hers.

Ben closed his eyes. He had to hurry up and get well, get his body and mind back under control.

He had seen something terrible in that young man's dark eyes tonight. But instead of concentrating on his Brotherhood obligations, all he could think about were soft gray-blue eyes and full, luscious lips twisted up in a wry smile.

Those kinds of thoughts could mean big trouble for a man dedicated to the Brotherhood. And more trouble was the very last thing he needed.

Chapter 2

Ben shifted his position in the hospital bed so he could look out the window. He saw the lavender-blue haze of dawn reaching over Beautiful Mountain.

Preparing to greet the daylight, Ben prayed—despite the fact his window view was west not east and the velvety navy nighttime was still clinging to the glass. Without seeing, he knew the Chuska mountain range would be next in line to receive the sun's warming gifts. Past there, the last place to receive the day's warmth would be the San Francisco Peaks, the westernmost of the four sacred mountains that made up the boundaries of *Dinetah* territory.

If he'd been at his home this morning, he would be up, blessing the rising sun with prayer and a pinch of pollen like all traditional Navajos. But just a glimpse of the familiar and beloved landmarks of his homeland gave him the strength he needed to get out of bed today. His head was splitting, but Hunter had sent a message through one of the nurses to say he would be coming by the clinic this morning.

Ben had no intention of lingering in bed when all he had was a slight concussion. He would talk to Hunter and then he would check himself out of here.

There was a war going on across his homeland, a secret war that had to be won. The only hope for the Dine to escape the terror of the evil ones was to be found in the hearts and minds of the warriors known as the Brotherhood.

Being a member of the Brotherhood, Ben understood his duty. He'd stumbled into a new threat last night—in the eyes of a teenage wrestler. And new strategies would have to be developed to head off whatever direction the evil Skinwalkers would be taking this time.

He eased an ankle to the side of the bed in preparation for lifting himself to a sitting position. Drawing in a deep breath, he threw both feet over the edge and rolled.

Tory was just reaching Ben's hospital door when she heard a loud grunt and then a thud. Those sounds were not good news, she knew. Picking up speed, she bounded through the door and skidded to a halt on the other side.

"What in the name of heaven do you think you're doing?" she demanded, as she raced over and knelt beside him on the floor.

He lifted his head and gazed at her with those bloodshot but remarkably sexy eyes. "Trying to get dressed so I can get out of here."

Sitting back on her heels, she watched him lift himself up on his elbows. Tory frowned at his shaky efforts. "As your physician, I insist you remain in bed for further observation. At least until you can manage to keep the floor under your feet rather than have it knocking you in the chin."

Ben put both his palms flat against the linoleum and tried to push himself into a sitting position. No luck. After several grunts and groans, his cheek was back resting on the cold, hard floor.

Feeling sorry for him, Tory tried to contain her smile as she slid her hands under his elbow and helped him to a sitting position.

"Okay," he muttered. "But getting me back to bed will not be so easy. I outweigh you by…a lot."

She grinned at him. "Perhaps so, big guy. But I have the moves. It's all in the use of leverage, you know." She fluttered her hands in front of his face, then cut the air with flat-handed karate chops.

Ben winced. "Can we just sit still a minute before we try anything that desperate?"

"Uh…for how long? It's not terribly comfy down here, and you should be back in bed."

"You can go back to work, Doctor. When my head stops spinning, I'll send out smoke signals."

Tory helped him to lean back against the gunmetal gray chest of drawers. "Sure. We can wait," she said with a smile, as she pulled a pillow off the bed and shoved it behind his back. "But I'll stick here, if you don't mind. Let's have a powwow. You supply the peace pipes and I'll supply the blood pressure cuff."

"Hmm," he muttered. But he closed his eyes and let her take his pressure.

His coloring was too pale, his breathing a little too shallow. But his blood pressure readings were good.

"Why is it so important for you to leave?" she asked in one of her best bedside manner voices.

He opened one eye to glare at her.

Instead of noticing how red-veined and unfocused that eye was, instead of making note of the puffy, black bruises under both his eyes that were about to become purple and green mountain ranges, instead of any of those more practical observations, when Tory looked at him all she could hear was her own heart beating like a kettledrum. Thunk. Thunk. Pound. Pound.

Good heavens. She was turning into a puddle of mush just by sitting this close to his heat, and by gazing into the intensely sexy depths of one dark brown eye.

"I have work to do," he finally told her.

"Yes, well, I'm sure your patients will understand. Doctors are only human. They can get injured, too."

"No," he said with authority. "I must do my duty. I must. It's a matter of life and death."

The way he said it made her nervous. People had always called her a workaholic. Especially her ex-husband, Mike, who'd eventually used that as an excuse to dump her.

But the truth was, she felt strongly about her responsibility to heal the sick and injured. She'd taken oaths, made promises. It was what she did. Who she was.

Ever since she'd been a young girl, the middle child with four brothers and all of them known as the poor kids whose mother had to work three jobs just to make ends meet, Tory had always been the one who tended to the others. She'd known enough about butterfly bandages, antibiotic salve and plaster casts by the time she got to med school that she could've applied the stuff blindfolded.

She could feel Ben's need to go back to work deep in her bone marrow rather than just understanding him on some intellectual plane.

"I'll make you a deal," she began, like a used-car salesman. "Twenty-four hours. Stay until tomorrow morning and I will go see your patients this afternoon. Today is my day off and if you—"

"Right after lunch," he interrupted. "I must be out of here by noon at the latest."

He'd deliberately ignored her offer, and his rudeness drove a tiny spit of anger down her spine. But then she remembered what April had said about him being a medicine man. Perhaps he knew his patients would refuse to see a white woman doctor.

Tory understood that a big part of what made a good doctor-patient relationship was respect and she decided not to push it. She'd worked long and hard to earn respect, and hoped to see it in patients' eyes when they looked to her as their physician. She had no intention of deliberately setting herself up to be treated badly.

Not even to help out the man in a hospital gown sitting next to her—who was right now giving off enough heat to buckle her knees and make her forget her oaths.

"All right," she said. "I'll split the difference with you. Twelve more hours. I'll come in before supper tonight and check on you. If you can stand by yourself then, I'll sign your release papers. I'll even drive you home."

He grunted, and opened both eyes in order to argue.

But Tory cut him off at the pass. "No arguments. That is my final offer. Take it or take it."

Ben sat for a moment, considering. "Are you off now? Will you go home and rest before you come back?" She looked exhausted and he knew that would be his chance for escape.

She nodded. "Yes, the day shift has come in. I'll go home in a few minutes. But you don't have any room to negotiate. And don't think you can sneak around me. It's a done deal."

Ben steadied himself and refused to say what he was thinking. If he felt well enough, he could check himself out of here any time. He didn't necessarily need to wait for her to come back.

"Fine," she said as she rose to her knees. "Now…"

The door opened and Officer Hunter Long of the Navajo Tribal Police stuck his head inside the room. His eyebrows rose when he spotted both patient and doctor on the hard floor. But Ben noticed he made no mention of their compromising positions.

Even though he was born half Anglo, Hunter had been raised in a traditional Dine home. And Ben knew it would've been rude for any traditional Navajo to acknowledge a social mistake or embarrassment.

"May I come in, Dr. Sommer?" Hunter asked.

"Yes, please, Officer Long. I could use your help."

Hunter came through the door and squatted beside Ben. *"Ya'at'eeh,"* he said in greeting.

"Atsili," Ben mumbled as an answer. "Now help me up off this damn floor."

Though Ben caught the laugh hiding in his twinkling blue eyes, Hunter managed to keep the smile to himself. But in two very clever moves, Hunter levered the dizzy patient back into his hospital bed. Ben gave him a grateful grunt.

"Thank you, Officer," Tory said. "I was afraid we might need to rent a crane to make that maneuver."

"Go home, Doctor," Ben groaned from his bed. "You've been hovering over me for hours. Get some sleep."

She turned and fisted her hands on her hips. "You think

I don't know what you're planning? Wrong." Leaning over, she straightened and fluffed his pillow. "You are under strict doctor's orders to stay put until I say so. I'm issuing a formal request to the tribal police right this minute. You are in no condition to drive and should be arrested if caught out on the roads today or tomorrow."

Okay, so he wouldn't drive. He would have to give that up soon anyway, for entirely different reasons. No problem.

"And," Tory went on, "I have already hidden your clothes. Anyone who brings you a change of clothing today will not be admitted to the clinic.

"I am going to get some sleep, Dr. Wauneka," she continued smugly. "I strongly suggest you do the same. We will revisit our arrangement before supper this evening."

Tory spun around on the slick linoleum floor, nodded at Hunter and stalked out of the door.

"Whew," Hunter murmured in Navajo a moment later. "That's some *bilagáana* woman you have there."

"She's not my white woman," Ben said with a rasp.

"Too bad. Nice legs."

"Can we not talk about Dr. Sommer now? Aren't we both still committed to the oath of the Brotherhood that demands each of us stay celibate in order to remain focused in our fight with the Skinwalkers?"

"My older brother has already made that oath obsolete," Hunter reminded him. "Kody is married now and yet he continues the work of the Brotherhood. What is good for one may be good for all."

Ben fussed and shifted in bed. "I disagree. Kody Long can be unconcerned about the possible consequences of having a weak link, but I'm not. I wouldn't like to someday wake up and find that my loved ones have been kidnapped or hypnotized in an effort to get to me."

Hunter put a hand on his shoulder. "All of us already have family we love in Dinetah, cousin. We fight the evil ones so that our families and clans will be safe. Not so we can avoid relationships."

Ben thought back to the original pact the men of the Brotherhood had made. In tales and legends, the ancient Navajo warriors were said to have remained celibate and neither ate nor drank before a raiding party. In Ben's mind, returning to tradition in every way was the only thing that could completely destroy the Skinwalkers and save the Dine from this terror.

But he didn't think Hunter would be up for a lecture at the moment. Waiting for a time when his head cleared sounded better, too. "Well, we should at least avoid the subject of Dr. Sommer for now. We don't even know if she's married or not."

"Not."

"You checked on her?"

Hunter shrugged. "I have a need to know the people I am expected to protect. In this war, there is no easy way of recognizing a foe before it is too late. So we must quickly be able to judge who is a friend."

Ben clucked his tongue. "There's over a hundred and fifty thousand Navajos living on the reservation...not to mention whites, Hopis and Mexican Americans who live in Navajoland, too," he reminded his cousin. "Do you intend to know them all?"

A smile came over the policeman's face. "No. Just the pretty ones.

"Dr. Sommer is exactly as she appears to be," Hunter continued more soberly. "She lives alone in a house owned by the clinic over on Bluebird Ridge. She's completed three months toward her three-year repayment duty to National Health Service. She has few friends here. No dates."

That was too much information about a woman who should not interest him, Ben thought. "Can we talk about what happened last night?"

"I thought perhaps you would rather avoid the subject of what put you in this hospital bed," Hunter suggested. Then he shook his head and lowered his voice. "You're supposed to be the heart and the spirit of the Brotherhood, not the muscle. Yet here you are with an injury."

"It's the muscle between my ears that is to blame," Ben admitted with chagrin. He had no intention of mentioning that he'd been distracted by the beautiful blond doctor. Especially now that he'd made such a big deal about not talking about her.

"Why were you at the wrestling match last night?"

"I've been giving checkups and sports medicine advice to the Owl Springs School team," he began. "One of the teens is the grandson of one of my patients. A few days ago he came to me and confided he'd heard a rumor that the Raven Wash team members have secretly been taking steroids. The Owl Springs boys were considering doing the same thing. They need a level playing field in sports. There are scholarships on the line, but only for winners."

"So you went to check out the Raven Wash team for steroid use?" Hunter questioned.

Ben nodded. "I never imagined that high school sports teams would have anything to do with our war. In helping them, I just wanted to do something for a change that would feel normal.

"We've worked so hard, trying to keep the evil ones' existence a secret from most of the Dine," Ben continued. "Sometimes I can even fool myself into thinking that a huge part of our world is still free from the evil."

Ben silently admitted to himself that such thinking was foolhardy. Just like his dream of leading a return to traditionalism was probably nothing more than a flight of fancy. In his opinion, though, going back to the old culture and original religious practices would be the only solid ways of beating the current threat.

"I know there are rumors circulating of Skinwalkers," Ben went on. "All around Navajoland. But I never expected to find…"

"What?"

"The boy that attacked me last night," he answered with a question of his own. "What happened to him?"

Hunter stuck his thumbs in his pockets and rocked back on his heels. "I had to use the Taser to subdue him. But when I went to cuff him, he'd stopped breathing. Paramedics pronounced him dead at the scene, but seemed positive it wasn't the stun gun that caused it. The FBI gets involved with all unnatural deaths on a federal reservation, of course. And they insisted on a full investigation and autopsy."

"Not your brother, the FBI agent, I take it?"

"No, not Kody. It was Special Agent Teal Benaly. She's new in the Gallup office."

"What did the family of the one who died have to say about an autopsy?" Respecting Navajo taboo, Ben did not ask or mention the name of the deceased.

"His family lives way back up in Big Sky Canyon with no phones or electricity. Supposed to be Yellow House People. But when an agent went up there to talk to them, the place was deserted. Neighbors hadn't seen them in weeks."

"Have you been suspended from the NTP?" Ben asked in a small change of subject.

Hunter nodded. "With pay. Pending the FBI investigation."

"There are things about the one who died that the FBI will not understand," Ben volunteered. "But I'll be interested in the autopsy results because I don't think he was on steroids or drugs of any kind."

"I'm sure the FBI will want to interview you," Hunter warned. "What are you going to tell them?"

"Not the truth." Lies were acceptable in traditional Navajo culture if they did no harm. *White lies,* the white man called them. Good name.

"What really happened, my cousin?"

"As he came at me, I looked that teen straight in the eyes, trying to throw him off balance." Ben didn't much like making that admission, but this was war. "I find it hard to believe he died of either drugs or Taser."

"Why?"

"There was Skinwalker evil lurking deep in those eyes. The enemy apparently has recruited a teenager to their side. Or…maybe they have found a way to turn themselves into other humans."

The ramifications of either possibility made Ben's skin crawl. It was horrible enough that Skinwalkers could turn themselves into animals with supercharged powers and had been practicing mind control. But if they could also change their images into whatever or whomever they chose…

"We need to notify the Brotherhood," Hunter said without hesitation. He turned and strode out of the room.

Ben closed his eyes and tried to rest. The Brotherhood needed a new plan. And he would give it some more thought.

Just as soon as his head stopped pounding—and just as soon as he stopped seeing soft, blue-gray eyes every time he closed his eyes.

Chapter 3

Ah. Her own quiet hideaway.

Tory had that same remarkable thought every time she unlocked her front door and stepped into the blessed peace of the rental house she had converted to her own special space.

She should be thinking of how to find the time to run errands. Her refrigerator contents were looking pretty lame. The tribal post-office employees had been begging her to come pick up her mail. And in another day or two, her dirty laundry pile would grow too big to fit into her car's trunk.

Tomorrow. All those domestic chores would wait another day. Right now she needed to take a bath, close the heavy blackout drapes and catch up on all the sleep she'd lost in the past twenty-four hours.

But the lure of the backyard drew her, the way it always did whenever she came home. Tory moved across the shiny hardwood floors of the one big room that made up her living room, dining room and kitchen.

She didn't stop to focus on the good mood that always settled over her in this space. Passing right by the cozy suede furniture, the fantastic built-in bookcase that covered one whole wall and the wonderful handwoven Navajo area rugs under her feet, Tory let the warm sensations soak right in. She felt tired but content as the sunny yellow paint that the hardware store clerk had called Anasazi Ochre soothed her.

Throwing her keys and purse on the kitchen counter, she undid the locks and opened the sliding glass door that led to the ten-by-ten cedar deck. She drew a breath of the crisp spring air into her lungs and decided the exhilarating oxygen on the rez must be addictive.

As usual, her gaze went straight to the top of the sandstone cliff that was her nearest backdoor neighbor. Tory loved her isolated yard and relished the small garden plot she'd set out for herself. But the towering red-and-gray spires of sandstone that the maps named Bluebird Ridge filled her with awe no matter how many times she saw them.

Whistling winds, the friendly springtime winds her neighbors had mentioned, skated merrily down the sides of the cliff and wafted across the yard, crooning their happy tune. Tilting her head, she listened and smiled.

Never once in her previous life had she stopped to notice the music in the sounds of life around her. Background noise had simply been there, in the bustling sounds of the city and the strained sounds of a houseful of kids or the halls of a busy hospital. But it had stayed just outside her consciousness.

Since moving to the reservation, she'd discovered her body liked the quiet of a natural setting. She sat down on the bottom step of the deck to let her mind rest while she checked out her planting beds.

Were those almost visible green tips, sprouting through the soil, the flowers she'd put into the ground? According to the seed salesman, it had been much too late to plant bulbs by the time she'd settled into the house after the first of the year. But she'd set out tiny prestarted plants for an herb garden and had poked wildflower and marigold seeds into the soil just a couple of weeks ago.

"Hello, friends," she said to the new baby plants. "I hope you like it here in my garden."

It seemed natural to speak to these growing things. But was she ever glad no one else was nearby to hear the one-sided discussion.

Her smile grew wider as she thought about her family and circle of friends back in Southside Chicago. None of them would've imagined Tory Sommer could possess a green thumb. But she'd discovered her own surprising love of the outdoors shortly after arriving in this very different part of the world. It seemed odd, the way the natural world had so suddenly become her sanctuary and her best friend.

She'd been born and raised in a tiny tenement apartment, and that was where she'd thought she belonged. Becoming a waitress or a factory worker like her mother wasn't something she would have to decide. It was what she'd been born to do, and green things were nowhere near her life.

Then she'd discovered medicine and from that moment on, she'd been positive that it would be her one true place in the world. It had been the only thing that called her name and had become the basic makeup of her being.

Unwinding the hose, she wondered if her newfound

love of the outdoors would now compete with medicine for her attention and time. Turning a refreshing splash of well water on her incubating garden, Tory smiled at the thought of mixing healing with gardening. The two things did seem compatible.

A second later another thought intruded, and she stopped picturing the way the spring garden would look with blooming flowers of every pastel hue. Instead of dreaming about gardens or healing children the way she'd done during many years of medical training, her thoughts turned to remembering a sensual look in a pair of penetrating eyes.

Eyes that belonged to Dr. Ben Wauneka.

His gaze probably made female patients swoon.

When she'd first seen him, his dark eyes had made her think of a clear midnight sky. It was as if her great new love of the outdoors had settled on his face and had seemingly spread out across his features for her exclusive enjoyment.

She would've had to be asleep or dead not to notice.

But had she noticed too much? It certainly had been a stronger reaction than she'd ever experienced with her ex-husband.

Tory had been far too occupied with finishing her residency to consider what had gone wrong between her and Mike. But three years had passed, and she barely remembered why she'd thought the two of them had ever belonged together in the first place. Mike, always the salesman, had simply swept her away, she supposed.

He'd been a slick up-and-coming stockbroker. She would be willing to bet that he'd just wanted a smart doctor wife to prove something to his clients. Or maybe to himself.

They had been mismatched from the start. She never

cared much about money, and couldn't seem to get it in her head that Mike's every move was ignited by greed.

When it was over between them, she hadn't lifted a finger to stop the no-fault divorce. Forcing money issues and settlements would've only dragged it out. But at the time she *had* wondered if losing him shouldn't have hurt more.

With a shrug of dismissal, she'd simply gone right back to work. Medicine interested her. Mike…not so much.

The thoughts she'd been having about getting closer to the sexy Native American doctor were also totally out of line. Talk about two people being mismatched.

The only possible connection the two of them could have in common was medicine. But if April had been right about Ben's secondary practice as a native medicine man, then they were a million miles apart on that subject, too.

Sighing, Tory bent to pluck something that looked like a weed, hoping to recognize one when she saw it.

Perhaps her body had also not recognized the truth when she'd first seen Ben. Lust seemed a surprising sin for her to have all of a sudden.

Nothing was familiar about it. In fact, everything in her new world seemed slightly off-kilter.

Looking down at the puddles around her baby plants, the only thing Tory felt sure of was that from now on, wherever she went, she would have to have a garden.

Not far away, the Raven and the Navajo Wolf stood sheltered in the shade of a clump of cottonwoods, watching as Tory rewound her hose and went inside. The day's shadows began to shrink around them as the sun moved higher in the sky.

The odd fact that these two shadows could disregard the

daylight didn't seem unusual to them anymore. There were many ways that their Skinwalker power had been growing recently. Changing over from human to their animal personas in broad daylight was just one more special power that they and their brothers could use in the Quest.

"Did this woman's meddling cause the loss of one of our newest Skinwalker recruits?" the Wolf questioned his lieutenant.

"Not at all," the Raven replied. "The 'changeover' powder you supplied was too potent for our young cult member. But there will not be any residue left in his body. The autopsy will show only a defective heart.

"The one who died took a double dose," the Raven continued with much trepidation. "Thinking to make himself stronger and more powerful than his opponents."

"Hmm. That he's dead is your fault, Raven. You are the one who is in charge of formulations and doses. Use the mind-control tricks I taught you to make sure all the young Dine follow orders. This one teenager was of no consequence, but I refuse to lose any of the others. The point is to build an army of young Skinwalkers to do our bidding."

Secretly quaking in fear at his boss's tone of voice, the Raven tried to change the subject. "You believe this white woman can be of use to us?" He knew the woman doctor, but had not considered her to be particularly special, and certainly of no worth in the Skinwalkers' campaign for money and power.

The Wolf growled, low and deep in his throat. "She can cause chaos by not knowing the Navajo Way, and she might distract the Brotherhood. That alone is worth some effort."

"But she is a medical doctor and might uncover what we are attempting to do with the young men. You want to try the mind control on her as we did with the other *bilagáana* woman? It didn't turn out too well then. These whites are too stupid to submit quietly."

Showing his fangs in a sharp move that disturbed the Raven's perch, the Wolf narrowed his eyes at his comrade.

"Use your human powers to control this one," he snapped. "Whites can be easily persuaded. Put fear into her heart and confuse her. That's all we require for now to cause the Brotherhood trouble.

"I need distractions and time," the Wolf continued. "Especially for the *Navajo* doctor, the one who tries to walk the line between traditionalist and modern culture."

"But his new illness…"

The Wolf waved off the Raven's concerns. "He has more power than most, power enough to reach beyond his disease and still cause us problems. I want him neutralized, and I intend to steal as much of his energy as I can."

"Dr. Hardeen wants to see you in his office, Dr. Sommer," Russel, the nurse-practitioner, announced before he spun and stormed down the corridor.

Uh-oh. Tory figured her boss would give her a lecture about going out alone after dark last night. Okay, she'd agreed with him that she would take no chances. But sheesh, she was tired and didn't need another boring lecture today.

She had hoped Dr. Hardeen wouldn't have returned yet from the tribal council meeting in Window Rock. No such luck. There wasn't anything to do but take it now.

Pushing loose strands of damp hair behind her ear, she put down Ben's chart and marched toward Dr. Hardeen's office. She'd overslept by an hour, dashed in and out of the shower and then drove like a madwoman to get here. And it was a little later than she had planned. But she'd been pleased to learn that Ben was already sitting up, dressed and waiting for her to sign him out.

First, though, Tory steeled herself to take Dr. Hardeen's lecture. She wasn't terribly happy to do so. She was a grown woman, a physician, and it irked her no end to be cautioned about going out at night.

Did her employer have the right to put her on some kind of curfew? Not in any circumstance that she could think of. But she warned herself to keep her mouth shut. She was a stranger to the ways of the rez, had signed a contract with the clinic to work here and had been lucky to find this way to pay off her loan.

The door to her boss's office was closed when she got there. She tapped lightly then pushed it open a few inches.

"You wanted to see me," she called out around the door. She waited to be acknowledged before walking in, but peeked past the door's edge anyway.

"What?" he said absently as he stood bending over his desk. Dr. Hardeen was apparently looking for something, but in a second he raised his chin and spotted her standing there. "Oh. Tory. Yes, come in. Come in."

Raymond Hardeen had to be in his early fifties. A soft-spoken man with thinning white hair cut short in a business style, he was often distracted but had a nice disposition. Tory liked what she'd learned about his background.

He had founded the Raven Wash Clinic nearly twenty years ago and had fought lengthy, difficult battles in order to obtain enough financing to run the place long-term. Today, the clinic operated on a combination of tribal money, private insurance payments and semipermanent federal Indian grants. The community owed him a huge debt of gratitude.

Along the way, Raymond Hardeen had also discovered his flair for politics and had run for the office of Raven Wash Chapter delegate to the tribal council. There were one hundred and ten chapters on the reservation. But Tory imagined that none of the others had a delegate who was quite so well-respected.

In her opinion, it was a good possibility that next year Dr. Hardeen would be elected president of the entire Navajo Nation. He made a terrific administrator.

"Have a seat, Tory."

She did as he asked, gritted her teeth and waited for the lecture. As much as she liked him, another of his advisories would be more than she could stand today.

"I see you were the attending for Dr. Ben Wauneka last night. I've been meaning to talk to you about him for a couple of weeks. Now seems a good time."

"About Ben?" And there would be no lecture?

"Wauneka is a competent physician, treating the People in an area where there has been no medical care in the past. He provides a much-needed service.

"And I like the guy, even though I think he's a bit of a hypocrite," Dr. Hardeen continued with a sigh. "He's one of those people who are enthralled with a romantic version of the Navajo past, and I'm not sure that's a good thing. It's people like him who tend to hold back progress. You know what I mean?"

Tory nodded but was beyond puzzled about what any of this might have to do with her.

"I want the Dine to move forward, not backward," Dr. Hardeen droned on. "We deserve the best that medicine and science have to offer. The People are descendants of an ancient civilization, far superior to most. They should have good jobs, quality education and the best health care."

Yes, Dr. Hardeen certainly made a good politician. Blah, blah, blah. Tory wondered how long he could continue this way, but she sat back and let him go on.

"You may or may not know it, but Ben Wauneka is more than an M.D. He's also a medicine man…one of the traditional crystal gazers."

"Yes, I had heard that, but…"

Dr. Hardeen smiled at her and his eyes crinkled up behind his reading glasses. "Good. But I'll bet you don't know he has a secret."

Of course she didn't know Ben's secrets. What business was it of hers? She straightened up, shook her head and bit the inside of her cheek to keep quiet.

"Dr. Wauneka is going blind."

"What? How do you know that? Are you his regular physician?" She'd checked Ben's pupils a half-dozen times in the last twenty-four hours. What had she missed?

Dr. Hardeen frowned. "No. That's just the problem. The man tells me modern medicine cannot help him. He only mentioned his condition to me in private because he is concerned about the welfare of his patients. But he apparently intends to do nothing toward a possible cure. I thought since you—"

"But I understood he uses modern medicine in his own practice."

"This is different," Dr. Hardeen told her. "If his traditional clients learned about the blindness, they would be most unsettled and might refuse to let him be their crystal gazer. It would appear that he had been witched, and they'd be afraid to trust him."

"Witched." Now that was really out of her realm of experience. "What can I do? What are the symptoms he's experiencing, and do you know what's causing the blindness?"

Dr. Hardeen shook his head. "He wouldn't talk about it. I don't even know if he's been to a specialist, but we can't let him go blind. Quite a few of his traditionalist patients up in the hills will only accept medical help from him. And the People must have access to his kind of medicine. They must. Anything less is unacceptable.

"Continue being his doctor," Dr. Hardeen insisted. "Befriend him. Maybe get him to quietly accept a competent medical specialist who could find a cure."

Dr. Hardeen threw out a few suggestions of what he thought might be a diagnosis with an offhanded wave of his wrist. She admired her boss greatly for being so dedicated and caring. But he must not comprehend what he was really asking her to do.

"I don't think Ben will listen to me," she hedged. "He hasn't been particularly happy for me to be his attending."

"Ah, but you are the only one he has let get close. That must mean something. Be creative. You'll think of some way. He'll need a follow-up examination for the head trauma in a few days, won't he?"

"Yes, probably. But…"

"Well, there you go. That'll be a good time to suddenly *discover* this other problem. In the meantime, be his friend. I'm convinced only a friend will be able to make him see the light and get some help."

Tory couldn't think of anything she wanted to do less. Getting close to Ben made her mind go all fuzzy and her body react with unusual stirrings. But Dr. Hardeen was adamant and refused to take no for an answer. When he wound down, he quickly dismissed her from his office, saying he had another meeting to attend tonight.

She needed this job to pay off her loan, and she liked her boss and wanted to please him. Meddling in someone else's medical problems seemed wrong, though, even if the reasons for it were right.

But every good reason aside, this was *Ben* they had been talking about. How could she manage?

"Dr. Sommer, may I talk to you a second?" The request came from over her shoulder as she hurried down the hall toward Ben's room.

She turned and found herself staring into odd, blank eyes. "I'm afraid I'm running late, Russel. What is it?" Just her luck that nurse-practitioner Russel was in charge again this evening.

"It's nearing sundown. Would you like me to find someone to drive home with you? Or are you planning to stay until morning again?"

"What is this big deal about the dark?" she asked irritably. "I don't get it. It sounds like you're all covering up a gang-related drug problem or something. Is it drive-by shootings that have everyone on edge?"

Russel moved closer to her and she had the urge to turn around and run. But she held her ground.

"There are worse things on the reservation at night than gangs, Doctor," Russel whispered, and she had to move even closer to hear him. "Horrors so unimaginable that the People dare not speak of them."

"Ghosts? Or the bogeyman?" she asked with a laugh. "Are you telling me that this whole don't-be-out-alone-at-night thing is all based on superstition?"

Russel grabbed her elbow in a viselike grip. "Do not make fun of things you can't understand. You might not have a chance for regrets."

That did it. Tory jerked her arm away from him and took a step back. "This had better not be some kind of threat. Dr. Hardeen wouldn't be pleased to hear about it."

The nurse-practitioner's black, slitty eyes widened. "No threat, ma'am." He took two steps backward. "But remember that it was me who tried to warn you." With the last word, Russel turned and rushed away down the corridor.

Tory mentally brushed herself off. What a pain in the ass. Dark or not, she intended to sign Ben's discharge papers and then drive him home. Ghosts. How imaginative.

She straightened her shoulders and continued on her way to check Ben. Damned if she was going to let either Dr. Hardeen *or* crazy nurse Russel waylay her any longer.

Chapter 4

"There's another one," Tory said.

Ben turned in the passenger seat of her car and stared straight ahead. "Another what?" He'd expected to see something flashing in the headlights, but there was nothing—nothing but blacktop and the familiar semidesert landscape of juniper brush and sage that told him they were nearing his home.

He'd been daydreaming. Well…dusk dreaming, anyway, and he hardly ever let his imagination go like that.

But it was easy having flights of fancy about *her*. She'd worn her long blond hair down this evening, and he'd been having visions of her rising above him, naked in the sunshine. He saw her in his head, with a cerulean blue sky outlining her silhouette and that fine golden hair like fire, as the wind whipped it around.

His inner spirit had recognized her from the first time

he'd seen those fantasy blue-gray eyes. Something about her. He'd known her. Had always known her. Throughout all time, perhaps.

But he realized those thoughts were just romantic nonsense. Though they were exactly the sort of thing that made him the most Navajo. He tried shoving them aside so his thinking would be clearer. The People were at war and any stranger was either the enemy or a bystander.

Either way, with her, he needed to forget the poetry and remain alert and focused.

"I think they must be wild animals of some sort," Tory said, breaking into his thoughts. "The first time I saw one, I thought it was a dog. But if these things are dogs, they're the scraggliest, wildest-looking dogs I've ever seen."

Ben sat up farther in the seat. "Where are you seeing these animals? Not up ahead or I would've noticed." His eyesight was worse than ever tonight, but still he certainly would've spotted animals in the road.

"In the rearview mirror."

Damn. That was the answer he had dreaded. "Lock your door, Tory."

"What? Why on earth…"

Ben reached around her and depressed the electric lock button that controlled every door. He heard the telltale click and took another breath. Her scent captured him, and he noted that even the musky smell of her seemed familiar.

"What is the matter with you?" she squeaked.

"The Dine have many legends and myths," he began calmly. "The stories have served us well over the millennium. Some of them might seem far-fetched and steeped in superstition to someone like you who has never tried to live in community with the natural world. But…"

"No, don't stop," she urged. "Please. I'd like to hear

what you have to say. Sometimes I feel that my patients would respect my advice more if I could communicate in a way that made sense for them. I'd like to know more about Navajo myths."

Of course she would, Ben thought. It was what he would do if their situations were reversed. But would she be willing to open her mind to all the possibilities?

"Did it occur to you that it should be hard to see animals in the dusk with no lights and without the benefit of your headlights? What you've been seeing is a coyote," he told her patiently. "The Dine have a long-standing love/hate relationship with the coyote. He's supposed to be a trickster. He causes all sorts of trouble, but not with a mean spirit."

Tory turned her head to glare at him. The look on her face told him she thought he had freaked out entirely.

He wished he didn't have to tell her anything. Ben had hoped they could just drive to his hogan without incident. He would've thanked her, made sure she had a secret escort from the Brotherhood and then sent her home. Doing anything else with her or for her would put too much temptation in his path.

But now he had no choice.

"Tory, don't take the things people on the rez tell you too literally. Just let the words float past you. If you listen with an open mind, sometimes…"

Tory stepped on the brake. "The ideas seep right into your bones." She finished his thought and turned to him. "That was what you were going to say, wasn't it?"

"Yes. Exactly."

She nodded. "I knew it. I said those same words about gardening and nature to myself just this morning."

"Then clear your head of city ideas and don't prejudge anything. I assume what you've been seeing is the

Navajo's mythical 'coyote' and he's come to issue a warning," Ben told her in a quiet voice. "But we had better keep going. The longer we stay exposed, the darker it becomes and the more vulnerable we are to attack."

"Attack? By whom?"

Ben shook his head. "Just drive, Doctor. We haven't got a lot of time."

Tory clamped down on the words that were itching to let loose from her mouth, put the car back into Drive and continued on down the highway. For several very good reasons, she needed to become closer to Ben. And not the least of those was her boss's request.

So telling Ben what she really thought of his odd warnings and his fanciful story about a coyote was not a smart idea. The man wasn't well. He had just survived a head trauma, and she knew he'd taken a painkiller right before they left the hospital.

It had probably been the drugs talking, anyway.

She kept her mouth shut and let him give her the complicated instructions toward his house. Glad she didn't have to follow a map and that she had a local guide, Tory found herself going west on a series of dirt roads that seemed to take them higher and higher in elevation.

The farther they went the worse the roads grew, until finally most stretches were nothing more than ruts cut through boulders and loose sand. Potholes loomed ahead of them like deep black holes in the universe. She did her best to stay out of the deepest ones, concerned that Ben's head injury would worsen with too many bumps and strains. And she was petrified that her ancient Volvo sedan would bottom out and they'd be stuck here for good.

Just then, she swerved again and fishtailed the car's rear end on a sandy patch. "Wow," she blurted as she grabbed the wheel and fought the slide. "You sure this is the right way? How do your patients find you way out here?"

"Want me to drive, Doctor?" Ben said with a chuckle.

"No, thanks. My driving may be rocky but I'm not the one taking meds. At least I won't drive us off the side of a cliff."

She might've expected him to make a smart remark back to that but he kept strangely silent. Wondering whether this would be a good time to mention his eyesight, she drove around a giant sandstone boulder and came to a wide, wooded bluff. To their right, the shoulder dropped off precipitously, and far below them the twinkling lights of distant farmhouses sparkled like the stars set in the growing indigo-blue sky above.

To the left, partially hidden by trees Tory couldn't identify, was a compound that included at least two structures that might be houses. A two-story barn with a series of fenced areas surrounding it sat well back from the other buildings.

"You can stop worrying about getting stuck on the road now. We're home," he told her.

She pulled in where he directed and, using the illumination from several outside electric lights placed high on poles around the property, got a closer look at the spot he called home. The biggest structure was obviously an A-frame house with floor-to-roof windows and an impressive cedar deck around the whole thing. It looked newly constructed and modern.

About twenty yards behind the house was one of the oddest-looking structures she had ever seen. "This must be your house. But what's back there?"

"It's a traditional eight-sided medicine hogan. My office."

"You're kidding?"

"Not at all," he said with a smirk. "You're doing it again, Tory. Stop judging until you know more about Dinetah. You may be surprised at what you learn."

"Sorry," she mumbled and reached for her door handle. "Wait a second for me to come around and help you out of the car."

"No," he said and held out his hand to stay her movement. "Turn off the car and let's just sit here a minute or two with the headlights off. It's better to be vigilant and safe."

"Better than what?" she asked but turned the car off anyway.

"Just give us a few minutes of silence, okay? I'll tell you the story some other time."

Once more she clamped her mouth shut. Both of them sat quietly in their seats and listened to the noises of the night. Off in the distance, Tory thought she heard an owl hooting. If she tried listening hard, she was sure she could hear the winds rustling in the trees around the house.

But other than that, there were no sounds at all. It was kind of spooky, this absence of noise, for a girl who'd been raised in the city. After a few minutes, Tory was absolutely positive she could hear the sounds of the stars shining and the noise of the blood pulsing through her veins.

"All right," Ben finally said. "It seems safe enough. Let's go." He flipped off his seat belt, opened his door and was outside the car before she could get her own door open.

"Wait a minute," she called after him. "Let me give you a hand."

Rounding the hood of the car, she ran full out to catch up, but he didn't turn around. Without hesitating, he started up the stairs to the front deck.

It was a good thing he had to stop to put his key in the

front door lock or she wouldn't have gotten to him in time. The minute she was directly behind him, she could hear him mumbling something that sounded like a singsong chant. It made her wonder for a second if the drugs he'd taken were giving him hallucinations. But she was positive the pain meds she'd prescribed could not possibly have that kind of side effect. So why…?

He opened the door, stepped across the threshold and flipped on an overhead light. "Forgive the lonely bachelor's mess in here. I wasn't expecting…"

Turning around to talk to her, his head was backlit by the light above and she almost missed the grimace. But she definitely caught the twinkle in those black-coffee-colored eyes. The eyes that had been haunting her senses ever since she'd first seen them.

"A gorgeous lady doctor who saves lives with the wave of her hand?" she supplied with a little laugh and a finger waggle, hoping to fill in the blank space in his sentence.

Ben barked out a quick laugh of his own and then winced again as the sound must've hurt his tender head. "Yeah," he agreed. "The same gorgeous lady doctor who *needs* saving from time to time. And who also causes a lot more trouble than she prevents."

"Oh, yeah? Well…" She was trying to think of a snappy comeback to his remarks. But her words were cut short when Ben turned, took a step and tripped over the edge of an area rug.

His feet came out from under him and he reached toward a nearby easy chair to break his fall. Before she knew it, Tory's street instincts took over and she ran in front of him, trying to keep him from landing flat on the floor. Her body managed the brunt of his weight just fine, but he was so overbalanced that it knocked them both backward to the chair.

Her knees buckled and she collapsed back into the cushions as the sexy Native American doctor landed right on top of her. She could tell by the inert and dead feel of the heavy weight of him that he was unconscious.

Not cool. There was no way she could ease a hundred and ninety pounds of dead weight off her body without taking the chance of injuring him. And there didn't seem to be anyone around to help her out with him this time.

"Ben…Dr. Wauneka, wake up. I need your help," she pleaded in his ear.

The sweat began to pour from her glands, and his warm breath against the wetness on her neck gave her the chills. He stirred slightly and the movement drove a whirlwind into her bloodstream.

All of a sudden her body refused to accept that the man on top of her was a patient—or a friend. All of a sudden he was simply a terribly sexy body. And *her* body was reacting to him in the way that came naturally between the sexes.

Her heart rate picked up speed, her breasts grew tender, and her senses went on hyperalert. Every breath he took mingled with the air coming from her own lungs. She got a whiff of hospital antiseptic mixed with a light scent of sage aftershave. But neither of them covered the more overpowering male musk that seemed to be dragging her under some kind of spell.

Oh, hell.

"Please, Ben. I can't take the chance of hurting you." The sexy female voice seeped through the fog in his brain.

"Then don't leave. Come to bed with me." The words sounded like they had come from his mouth, but could he have actually said such a thing?

Her quick intake of breath did more to bring him to his senses than anything else. The distraction of the soft body with rounded curves lying under him ceased to be all-consuming as he came to consciousness with a start.

"Excuse me?" She shoved lightly at his shoulders. "You have to help get yourself back on your feet. I could roll you off to the floor, but I'm afraid you might hit your head again."

He shifted slightly then bent his knees. Once he felt the carpet, he levered himself off her.

"That's a trick I'd love to see," he said as his hand automatically went to his eyes. "Sorry. Must be the pain medication that's making me dizzy."

Tory jumped out of the chair and stood, bending over him. "Come on. Try to stand. I'm here to lean on."

The smile came involuntarily. He only wished he could do more than lean on that luscious body. But he'd already managed to say something foolish. So he shut up, took her hand and stood up.

"There," she whispered. "Still dizzy?"

"No, Doctor. I'm just great now." He backed away from her close inspection, though his smart mouth seemed bent on self-destruction. "But we can roll on the floor if it would make you happy."

She propped her hands on her hips. "I don't believe the meds caused that fall at all. I think you didn't see the edge of the carpet and then pretended to be out cold to save yourself some embarrassing questions."

Not going there, pretty lady, he told her in his mind.

"Whatever you say, Doc." He decided to make a joke and change the subject. "It was sure fun falling on you, though."

Turning, he headed for the kitchen, flipping on lights

as he went. "You hungry? I'm not sure what we'll find in the refrigerator. But it's bound to be better than the clinic food."

"You sit down," she said and pointed toward the kitchen table. "I'll fix you something to eat before I go."

"Go? You can't leave tonight."

She opened the refrigerator door and stood with her back to him. "I'll make sure you're safely in your own bed first. And I'll come back in the morning to check on you if need be. But I expect that by sunrise you'll be fine."

"I'm fine already. That's not the point. It's just plain dangerous for you to be out by yourself at night." He took a second to pull out a chair and sit down, trying to decide what else to tell her. "And you'll never find your way back down the mountain in the dark, anyway. Stay here. Wait for daylight."

Traditional Navajos were trained to be patient. A quiet silence in the middle of a conversation that gave the other person time for consideration and contemplation before answering was only natural among the People. But Ben had noticed that silence seemed to make most Anglos nervous. They must have some basic gene flaw in their makeup that urged them to fill up every dead space with a lot of words.

Tory spun around with a carton of eggs in her hand. "Explain to me what could be so darned dangerous about driving in the countryside at night."

Instead of being quiet and giving Ben time to consider his answer, she let her own words pour out and fill up the silent air. "I'm sure it must have something to do with that legend you started to tell me about on the drive up here. Like the coyote tale, right?

"Well, where I'm from there is real danger on the

streets at night," she continued babbling. "Real bullets are shot from real guns. Gangbangers kill to protect turf and issue warnings to other gangs. And real people...real kids sometimes...get caught in the crossfire."

"What city is that, Tory?"

"Where do you keep your skillets?" She asked her own question before interrupting herself with his answer. "Chicago. Southside, actually."

He didn't know a lot about the Chicago area. But from what he understood of the ethnicity of the Southside, the woman must have stood out like the first cactus rose in spring. "Pans are in the drawer under the stove. Do you come from a big family?"

"Uh-huh. Four brothers and a second-generation Irish mother." She pulled out the pan she wanted and slammed the drawer shut with her toe. "In case you don't know, that means more aunts, uncles and cousins than you could hope to count. Dozens. Hundreds maybe."

"Are they all as fair-skinned as you?"

That question stopped her for a fraction of a second. "There's a tiny bit of Black Irish way back in a distant generation that spills out every now and then. But not in our immediate family. Every one of us is either a blonde or a redhead and we burn within ten minutes of being in the sun."

He chuckled at the image of how different she and her family were from him and his family. "Probably hard to find sunscreen on the rez. Do you wear a lot of hats?"

She laughed and turned on the burner under the pan. "I buy sunscreen by the caseload. Have it shipped in. And I try to remember to wear a hat when I'm in my garden."

Glad to be on an entirely different subject, Ben knew they would eventually have to revisit the conversation about her staying put overnight. There was no way he could let her go on her own until daylight. Especially not since the coyote had seen fit to warn them of the danger.

Giving it some thought while he listened to her talk about how different having a garden was from serving midnight shift E.R. rotations at Cook County Hospital, Ben found himself wondering why the Skinwalkers would want to either frighten or do injury to an Anglo doctor with no money and no power. It didn't seem logical.

"So…no one else lives here with you? No family or a significant other?" She set down two plates full of scrambled eggs and toast and started pulling open drawers, looking for forks.

"Second drawer from the sink," he pointed out. "And no. I live alone."

She had just given him a brilliant idea that was bound to work. "That's a good point," he said after taking his first bite of toast. "There isn't anyone who can come sit with me tonight, either. You really need to stay here in case I get up from bed, get dizzy again and fall."

Smiling, he watched her mull that over in her head. "If I ended up on the floor, I might lie there for hours and not be able to get up," he added for good measure. "I know you wouldn't want to worry about me all night."

She sighed and set down her fork. "There isn't anyone in the family who could come over? I thought all Navajos had families that were bigger than our Irish-American ones. Something about clans and traditions, isn't it?"

"I was an only child." He shrugged at her questioning look. "My mother died while I was off the rez at Yale med school. And my father decided he would rather live in his mansion in Santa Fe than live in Dinetah without her.

"I have plenty of cousins, of course," he added. "You're

right about Navajo clans. But…um…none of them would be willing to drive all the way out here until daylight."

It was a small lie. His cousins in the Brotherhood were not afraid of Skinwalkers and any of them would come if called. But the lie was worth telling if it kept her here and out of harm's way until morning.

"All right. All right," she said with a shake of her head and a tiny laugh. "I'll stay. But you had better have a comfortable couch."

"The sofa is okay." Those should've been enough words. He'd won and she was staying so he should've shut up while he was ahead. "But I'm more than willing to share my king-size bed with you instead if you like."

The idea had been percolating in his gut ever since he'd woken up to the feeling of her body beneath his. And it suddenly seemed to have a lot of interesting possibilities.

He held his breath while he waited for her to answer, knowing full well what she would say. Yet he couldn't stop himself from hoping he would be wrong this time.

In fact, Brotherhood vow or not, he had never before in his life wanted so badly to be wrong.

Chapter 5

Something disturbed Tory's sleep. Groggy from a strange dream that was even now fading from her consciousness, she rolled over on the couch and tried to decide where the sound had come from.

Had Ben called her name? Did he need help?

Looking toward the wide picture window at the soft gray light of predawn, she listened intently for any noise that might seem out of place. The first sounds she heard were birds calling in the distance. Pleasant and friendly. Tory decided she could get used to hearing that kind of noise first thing in the morning.

Then she caught a slight change in the sharpness of the birdcalls. Or maybe it was the wind, changing directions and stirring through the trees with a sound like a nearly inaudible mumble.

Sitting up, she slid her feet into the pair of Ben's old

moccasin slippers that he'd lent her last night. Then she pushed back the blanket and stood up. She'd meant to go listen at his bedroom door for any sounds of distress, but mumbling winds were a curiosity she just had to check out first.

Feeling a little chilled, she swung the multicolored blanket over her shoulders and clopped toward the front door. On the way, she used the growing daylight to admire the front room of Ben's house. With its soaring ceiling, its stuccoed fireplace and its expensive-looking suede-and-wood furniture, his home was modern yet cozy at the same time.

Nice place for a man she was coming to like more and more. He was intelligent, with a quirky sense of humor she found especially endearing, and was so damned sexy she found it hard to concentrate when they were together. That embarrassing self-revelation pulled a small sigh from her mouth.

When she reached the front door, she was surprised to see it had a frosted glass insert with some kind of scene etched right into the diffused glass. She didn't remember that from last night. Tilting her head, she made out a tree branch with the silhouette of a couple of large birds. And the whole vista appeared to be surrounded by leaves—or maybe bushes.

Again. Very nice. The words *understated elegance* ran through her head. She'd never really known what that could mean before. Now she did.

Reaching for the doorknob and intending to ease open the lock, she discovered it was already unlocked. Odd. She definitely remembered flipping the bolt behind them after they came inside last night.

She held her breath and as quietly as possible pulled open the door, preparing herself for the worst. A break-in?

The air whooshed from her lungs as she took a good look at the sight that greeted her on the other side of the door. It was her dream, or almost.

Ben stood at the edge of the front deck with his back to her. He faced east, at the sun's first tender rays of peach and yellow as they peeked over a distant mountain.

Naked from the waist up and with his ebony hair streaming down his shoulders from under a pale blue sash around his forehead, he seemed to be chanting something—or perhaps those were whispered prayers. He raised his arms and sprayed a dark blue substance into the wind. When he did that, the copper-colored skin tightened across his back as the ridges and bulges of muscles rippled with his every move.

Holy Mary, Mother of God. Tory had never been desperate to have a man touch her, take her. But seeing Ben looking so male and virile, that was all she could imagine.

Parts of last night's dream soared back into her brain. The images came fast and furious in lightning-like flashes. Ben, with his hair just this way and with his face decorated in odd bright lines of paint, carrying her up to the top of a rock-strewn mountain.

Another flash and she remembered the danger. Something had been chasing them up the side of that mountain. Snarling fangs, yellow eyes. A big dog or maybe a wolf.

She remembered an echo of fear. But the safety and protection she'd felt in Ben's arms blocked everything else as he'd bent to sear a kiss across her lips.

Whew, boy. She needed to get a grip on her emotions

here. Ben was no noble savage, and it was not likely they would be chased up any cliffs.

He was a dedicated physician who could be facing total blindness. And, by the way, she was no wilting heroine who needed rescuing, either.

Shaking her head to disperse the last remnants of the dream, Tory took a step and straightened her spine. Right now she had to breathe in reality, put aside the nagging lust created by the dream and move into the morning light to stand beside him.

Ben had heard Tory open the door behind him. But he didn't want to turn until he had finished the last part of his morning ritual prayers.

It was probably time for them to have a conversation about medicine men and Navajo traditionalism. Might be a long discussion. At least he hoped she would stick around long enough to hear him through.

"What was that blue feathery substance you were throwing into the wind?" Her low, smooth voice was softer than ever this morning.

He turned to answer, but she wasn't looking at him. Instead, Tory stared out at the view across his beloved Dinetah valleys and canyons. Under the Navajo blanket that was covering her hair, her face glowed with the rosy yellow rays of the rising sun. Radiating with health and with goodwill written right into her expression, she was the most beautiful vision he had ever beheld—except for the one that lay several thousand feet below her.

Waiting a second for his heart to start up again, Ben tried to think of a way to get around to everything he wanted to tell her.

"Uh...I was saying traditional morning prayers. And I

was spreading blue pollen…from wild larkspur. It's sacred to the Dine. Used by medicine men in many of our ceremonies."

"Oh? So being a medicine man is more of a religious calling than it is being a healer?"

He knew what she was asking and the answer she was hoping to hear. She was having trouble reconciling her Anglo medical training with traditional Navajo beliefs. Every time she looked at him, he knew she was wondering how he could possibly take part in superstitious and probably savage healing ceremonies when he also had a medical degree.

Well, it wasn't quite as simple as if he'd been an Anglo part-time Christian minister and full-time pediatrician. But he wanted to explain as much as he could. He knew she needed to understand.

She had said she wanted to be able to treat her patients here on the rez with the respect of knowing their traditions. He just hoped he would be able to bridge the wide gap in knowledge between them well enough to give her a glimmer of the truth.

"Walk with me for a few minutes," he said instead of giving her an immediate answer. "There's some things I want to show you."

He stepped off the deck, turned back and reached a hand out to help her down. The blanket slipped around her shoulders as she smiled and took his hand. Tightening her grip on the blanket with the other hand, she jumped down beside him.

Somehow he had missed how small-boned she was. Tory wasn't exactly tiny. Probably five foot five or six, she was of average height for a white woman. But as he held her slender fingers with his own and she walked quietly beside him, he couldn't help but notice her slim build.

Ben had no doubt that she had all the right curves in all the right places. Though so far she had kept them mostly hidden behind men's jeans and work shirts or heavy white lab coats at the clinic. But the way his body had reacted to her nearness, he was positive she was all woman under those clothes.

As he'd taken her hand, there had also been a strange shimmer of protectiveness lying in wait under his normal testosterone levels. A dash of male ego gripped his heart with tender tendrils, demanding that he watch out for her, no matter what else came between them.

They rounded the side of the house just as a big black bird swooped low enough over their heads to lift strands of their hair by the breeze from its wings.

"What the heck was that?" Tory asked as she swung around trying to see where it had gone.

"A crow, or maybe a raven," he answered. "Too big to be a common grackle." And he didn't much like the way the bird was behaving.

Tory dropped his hand while she looked around. But he noticed she inched in closer to him.

"Why would it fly at us like that?"

"It's spring," he began. "So maybe that was a momma bird, warning us off its nest."

But Ben had never heard of a crow or a raven doing such things. Now if that had been a mockingbird, it would've made more sense.

He heard a loud cackle and both he and Tory turned their faces upward to see the huge raven sitting at the pinnacle of his roof. Staring at them with nasty blue-black eyes and screaming with loud, mean shrieks, the raven appeared quite dangerous.

Tory shivered under her blanket beside him. "That bird

doesn't look like he cares for us much. The way he keeps staring is kind of creepy."

Ben agreed. But he wasn't about to tell Tory any such thing and scare her for no reason.

"The Bird People are friends of the Dine," he said instead with a forced smile. "We have spent thousands of years living as neighbors between the sacred mountains. I'm sure this one is just trying to protect his loved ones."

Tory threw him a glance with an expression on her face that said she couldn't believe he had just spouted such nonsense. But before he was forced to step any further off the nonsense cliff, a couple of red-tailed hawks strafed the raven's position on the roof. A squawking battle took place high above their heads and in a few seconds all three of the birds flew off in the direction of the Chuska mountains.

Saved from sounding foolish by a couple of true friends, Ben silently thanked the Bird People for their kindness. The sight of the dangerous-looking raven had made him wonder if the Skinwalkers could've discovered a way to change over to their animal forms in the daylight. If so, it was another new and disturbing piece of information for the Brotherhood.

"Wow. That was cool," Tory said. "Did you see that fight in midair?"

"There are many fascinating things in nature," he told her with authority—as if he knew exactly what he was saying and wasn't just as surprised by the raven as she had been. "Come on. Let me show you a few more."

"Oh, my gosh. Your garden is just wonderful." Tory heard herself gushing on, but sounding like a kid in the candy aisle didn't seem to be bothering her self-esteem any.

When she and Ben had walked to the back of his house, the first thing that had caught her attention was the small but lush garden that lay between his back door and the medicine hogan. She had never seen so many colors of lusty green, and silver, and…

"Are these all vegetables and herbs? They look so healthy. Fabulous. Just fabulous. I'm jealous of your gardening talents."

Kneeling in the freshly tilled earth, Tory stuck her nose right into the middle of a bush with prickly, purple-tipped leaves. One deep breath and she was hooked on the wonder of it all. Everything smelled basic and homey and—and safe.

Ben stood over her with a smile on his face. "This isn't a kitchen garden, Tory. No vegetables, I'm afraid." He put a light hand on her shoulder and she felt the zing bouncing off her spine as it slid down to the very core of her femininity—at approximately the center of her womb.

"*Hataaliis* are required to use specific minerals, herbs and specialty plants for the various ceremonies," he continued. "These are a few of the herbs we can grow domestically."

"*Hataaliis?*"

"Medicine men. I don't do many ceremonies myself. These days each *hataalii* has his own specialty because the ceremonies are so long and involved. My particular specialty is diagnosing illness. I'm called a crystal gazer.

"It goes along well with my GP practice," he added. "But I do treat many of the minor illnesses and injuries I see in my practice with natural remedies. It's familiar treatment for my traditional patients and they don't have to go all the way to a big clinic for the simple things. The remedies I use work better than most of the prescribed drug treatments anyway. Lots cheaper, too."

"Such as…?" She wasn't entirely hostile to the idea of

natural plants and herbs being useful in treating disease. The professor of one of her pharmacy classes had predicted more and more substances discovered in nature would be found to be better cures than the synthetic ones. And she remembered as a tiny girl that her Irish grandmother had used several natural remedies which seemed to work just fine.

Ben squatted down beside her. "See that tall leafy plant tied to a stick and covered over by a gauze shade? That's a special type of tobacco that grows in the mountains in Dinetah. Once the leaves are dried and then soaked to make them soft, they turn into a terrific poultice. Takes the infection right out of cuts and scrapes. And it doesn't leave the patient more susceptible to new strains of bacteria the way using too many antibiotics can."

Fascinating. But she wished he didn't have to tell her about it with his body in such close proximity to her own. She was finding it ever more difficult to concentrate—and breathe—around him.

His masculine scent had already permeated her skin and had entered her bones. If he didn't move away soon, his essence would be going through her veins and she would be lost.

Tory sat back on her heels, stunned at that last crazily poetic thought. What was the matter with her? She never thought about people or situations in such fanciful terms.

She promised herself to overcome the problem of Ben so she could think clearly again. And she would—just as soon as he backed away and stood up.

He pointed out a few more of the plants and their uses. The curly-leafed plant that when boiled tasted like camomile and could be used for babies' colic. The poisonous snakeweed that was great when used topically for ant or snake bites.

Wanting to learn them all, Tory listened as intently as was possible while he remained beside her.

Finally, when she could bear it no longer, she stood up and brushed off her hands. "Do you think I could manage to grow some of these things myself? I'm a real novice gardener."

Still squatting in the dirt, Ben silently glanced up at her and smiled. Two ideas came into her head in that instant. First, she suddenly recognized that he could barely see her, even from this close a distance. And second, her heart skipped a couple of beats at the warmth of his smile.

Both ideas would bear a lot more thought. Some other time.

"I don't see why not, if you're interested enough to learn how." He stood and lightly gripped her elbow.

She wasn't sure if his move was designed to help her ease out of the garden patch without knocking over any of the plants. Or if *he* was the one that needed someone to guide him as they walked through the obstacles.

But it didn't much matter either way. The energy traversing her skin, coming from where his hand was touching her elbow, was so different than anyone else's had ever been and felt so pleasurably commanding that she began to worry it might easily become a habit.

They crossed a grassy few yards and stopped where she could get a good look at the medicine hogan. "Interesting building design."

"Another tradition. The hogan must be an eight-sided building, measuring exactly so many feet by so many. It could be made out of logs or sticks, I suppose. But these stuccoed cement bricks are fine as long as there is a regulation smoke hole in the roof and the front door faces east."

"Smoke hole?"

"For the last few generations, it's been okay that the hole has been filled by a stovepipe to carry the smoke away. It's handy having a wood-burning stove in there to keep the place warm in winter and so I can boil the herbs when I need them."

Did that mean there was no electricity in his office? Hmm. Tory did not like the sound of that. Unsanitary, at the very least.

"I love the colorful blanket you've used over the entryway. But—"

"You're wondering about the electricity and plumbing, aren't you?" he interrupted. "Yes, I cheated and put them both in, but I try to make it as unobtrusive as possible for my elderly patients who don't expect it.

"The blanket was designed and woven by my cousin's grandmother. Lucas Tso made these turquoise bracelets I wear. And he's also a medicine man. But mainly he's a world-famous silversmith and a renowned Navajo artisan."

Ben crooked his head like he was studying the blanket's design for the first time. "In reality, that's covering a wood door. Another cheat. But the door is a must for keeping in the air-conditioning during the summer."

"Air-conditioning?" she asked with a chuckle. "I'd guess you probably really are cheating with that one."

"Yeah," he said absently. "But it sure comes in handy when I'm delivering babies. Just can't seem to get enough of a cross breeze when things heat up that much."

Tory couldn't keep the laugh from bubbling up and out of her mouth. She was afraid of sounding like a giddy teenager, laughing at every word he said.

"You deliver babies in this remote location all by yourself? Isn't that dangerous...and complicated?"

His eyes twinkled but his face remained sober. "I keep careful track of my pregnant patients' progress. If the pregnancy looks complicated or potentially dangerous, I send them to the hospital a week or two in advance of the due date and induce labor. Doesn't happen too often, though. Most of these women are hardy. Having babies comes easy.

"And as for performing the delivery all by myself," he continued, "I can only wish it were that simple. Usually, there are enough female relatives and midwives in attendance and crowding the room that I can barely get a chance to check either the mother's or the baby's heartbeats before the whole thing is all over."

"But if the delivery presents a surprise complication..."

"Then I'm attending and prepared. I haven't lost either a mother or a child yet. Only one time have I actually had to call in a medevac helicopter to rush a baby to ICU. And that was when the mother slipped and fell off a stepladder in her kitchen when the baby was just twenty-eight weeks along. But we managed to save that stubborn little girl. She's my patient now, too."

Ben pushed aside the gorgeous blanket and opened the door, allowing Tory to step inside ahead of him. A whole new world spread out before her. She'd been in every kind of doctor's office, hospital room and clinic in existence. At least she thought so. But none of them had looked like this one.

Within thirty seconds, after her eyes grew accustomed to the lower light level of the halogens, she had assured herself that the place was antiseptically clean. But there was no reception area. Patients stepped right into an exam room.

Lining the walls and hanging from the ceiling were an assortment of dried plants and shelves with bottles full of strange-looking crystals. It seemed odd, but it smelled wonderful in here.

Toward the rear of the octagonal room stood a series of carved wooden screens. She hoped they hid changing rooms and a bathroom with real plumbing where the doctor could wash his hands.

"Where do the patients and their families wait to be seen?"

"Usually we don't have enough of a rush to make any patient wait for diagnosis and treatment. But the families can wait on those benches outside along the walls and under the shade of the overhang."

She hadn't noticed benches. Maybe she was still lusting after the handsome doctor a little too much to see what was right in front of her eyes. Somehow her attention needed to be diverted back to reality. And soon.

As he showed Tory around his office, Ben tried not to give her a lecture on cultural sensitivity. But he caught her skepticism and knew she was wondering if it was really necessary to work so hard to integrate Dine culture into a medical practice.

It definitely was necessary. Most of his patients would refuse treatment from a strictly Western medicine practitioner. They would get medical treatment from someone who understood their culture and their needs, or they would not be treated at all.

Hoping Tory was open to learning, he knew she could be a big service at the Raven Wash Clinic if she would do a few things differently. And perhaps she would also learn enough to be able to help out here in his clinic when it became necessary.

As his eyesight worsened, he'd hoped *someone* would step in, at least part-time, to help his patients.

It was getting harder and harder to ignore and work around the haze and darkness that characterized his eye disease. Ben wondered how he could begin to approach the subject of his ever-increasing blindness.

He had grown to like Tory, even above his body's fruitless hormonal lusting. She was intelligent, curious and caring. And he strongly suspected she would want to make sure every patient, no matter how traditional or remote, received the treatment they required.

Fairly sure he could get Ray Hardeen to lend her out to his clinic on a part-time basis, Ben's only big question was whether she was flexible enough and willing to work hard enough to learn the traditions before his time completely ran out.

Or—whether he could stick with his Brotherhood vows of celibacy long enough to teach her.

Chapter 6

Stepping back out into the dazzling high-altitude sunshine, Tory crossed the medicine hogan's threshold a second before Ben did. But she heard the scuffling noises behind her back and knew he had tripped again.

Swinging around, she dropped the blanket from her shoulders and prepared herself to stop his fall this time. But instead, she found him still upright. He was hanging on to the door and its frame with both hands.

"Are you okay?" She stepped to his side and gripped his elbow, steadying him and letting him get his balance.

"Um…yeah," he hedged. "Let's sit on the bench and talk a few minutes before we go back to the house. Okay?"

"Sure." She wanted to give him an opportunity to save himself embarrassment. They would chat for a minute. But then she would insist on some answers about his eyesight.

After they were seated atop the blanket on the surprisingly comfortable wooden benches, she waited for him to start talking.

"Why'd you decide to become a doctor, Tory? Was someone from your family in medicine?"

She chuckled at the very idea. "Not hardly. I was the only girl in a family of boy athletes. My father died when I was eight." In fact, he'd dropped dead of a heart attack right in front of her eyes, but she didn't think it was necessary to go into the melodramatic details.

"My mother had to start working three jobs just to make ends meet." The memory of how she had never cried, not once, tried to interfere with her story but she refused to give it the time.

"I had to become the mom to my brothers. Fixing the dinner and washing our clothes was the easy part. But it took me a while to get the hang of bandaging cuts and soothing bruises. By the first time I entered a hospital emergency room, I knew that being one of the good guys in the white coats was what I was meant to do.

"I guess I'm just a natural-born healer," she added with a small laugh. But it was a revelation from a place buried so deep it surprised even her.

Ben sat for a moment and let her last thought drift away on a mountain breeze. Again, Tory decided to wait for him to speak first before she interrupted with questions of her own.

"I became a doctor because that was what my father wanted me to do," he finally said. "Well, that's not entirely true. I guess he would've preferred that I go into the oil and gas business with him. But my mother was a traditionalist. It horrified her when he sent me off the rez to attend boarding school. To a traditionalist, the Dine should always remain within the four sacred mountains of our homeland. To leave invites the bad spirits in."

He shrugged and smiled. "I did well in an Anglo school, but she always wanted me to come home and apprentice as a traditional medicine man. That would've been her way of paying off the evil spirits on account of my leaving, and then making things right again.

"In a small effort to make peace with her," Ben went on, "my father agreed that if I wanted to go to an Anglo med school, he would pay for it and I could spend my free time back on the rez learning the medicine men ceremonies."

"It must have been hard to be caught in the middle like that."

Another shoulder shrug told Tory that he would rather not talk about the emotion of that time.

"Was your mother pleased when you got your degree and came home?" Tory began to sense this conversation was getting too personal for either one of them.

"My mother died during my first year of med school. Her doctors said it was diabetes-induced heart disease, but the truth is far different. She died of a broken heart and from worrying that the worst possible consequences of my leaving would befall her clan."

"So you became a medicine man and now do both as a tribute to your mother?"

"Sort of. Except I've found I have an aptitude for doctoring. Like you, I feel I was born to be a healer.

"But it's more than that. There are some terrible things that have been happening to our clan and to the whole of Dinetah in the years since my mother died. And I believe it's my duty to help the People get back into balance. To right the wrong my leaving the sacred land has caused."

The conversation had just turned weird again. Too personal and altogether too strange for her.

She jumped up and pointed toward his garden. "Look. One of the plants is losing its leaves. And the poor thing has fallen over. Hold on a sec."

"Tory…"

Needing a minute, she left him sitting on the bench and waded out into the inviting green of the garden.

It wasn't enough that she was in lust for the first time in her entire life. But to find herself sinking into love with a man who on occasion sounded bipolar was beyond her imagination.

How had she gotten to this point? Was it some sleight of hand that he had mastered? Or was it some quirk in her own makeup that made her fall for men who were unavailable and all wrong for the long haul?

There didn't seem to be any possibility of saving herself from the heartache, though. She knew it deep in her gut—in that place where the instincts she had always relied on to save her stayed close to the surface.

There, Tory found the sure sense that she would gladly do whatever he needed. And knew she would do whatever it took to stay near him, helping him, until at last, he sent her away.

It was bound to happen that way. She was well aware that she did not belong here in his world forever.

Emotion was making her hands tremble, but she found a dried twig in the dirt and used it to prop up the injured plant. Not stopping to think about what she was doing, Tory dripped water from a bucket onto her new patient and on a few surrounding plants that looked wilted.

Absently, she crooned an old Irish lullaby to the tiny buds while she tried to sort out her feelings for the man who had planted them. But there could be no itemizing of her emotions. They were what they were. She was hopeless.

Ben's eyes picked that moment to leave him temporarily blinded. He sat quietly in the shade and used his other senses to imagine her in the garden. But soon he heard her crooning what sounded a little like the chant his mother had sung to him as a boy.

Tory was singing to plants? The idea made him smile.

In a few minutes she was back sitting beside him. Her warmth comforted him as his eyesight gradually returned.

"Is one of those out-of-balance things you mentioned your eye disease?" she inquired abruptly.

"What were you singing a minute ago?" He'd blurted out the question, hoping to distract her enough to avoid the discussion. But he knew he'd have to tell her eventually anyway.

"What? Oh. An old Irish lullaby my grandmother used to sing to me. She died when I was about five, but I keep finding myself singing it whenever I'm trying to soothe…

"Hold it," she said with a scowl he was glad his eyes could see. "Answer the question, please."

A quick shake of his head told Tory he was about to deny anything was wrong, but she raised her hand to stop him. "No use lying about it to me, Ben. I'm a doctor. And I'd like to be your friend."

"Ray Hardeen told you I'm going blind, didn't he?"

"He mentioned it. But I would've seen it for myself eventually anyway. I've been trained to spot the symptoms in children who can't vocalize their problems.

"You're not a child," she continued, chastising him as casually as she dared. "Why haven't you sought a diagnosis?"

"There is no cure, Doctor."

Her mouth dropped open and it took her a second to get the questions out that were forming in her head. "You've been to an ophthalmologist? What's the diagnosis?"

Ben leaned his elbows on his knees and stared down, absently, at his clasped hands. This would be the first time he had said the words aloud. Up to now, he'd managed to harbor the hope that it had all been a bad dream. Once it was out in the open, that hope would fade right along with his vision.

"The ophthalmologist I consulted in Albuquerque has convinced me it's a condition known as *azoor*," he told her. "It's rare, I guess. But the pathology is caused when the retina at the back of the eye malfunctions due to inflammation. The symptoms include—"

"Flashing lights and an enlarged blind spot," she interrupted. "I took a class in rare eye diseases as an elective. From what I remember of this one, the area of visual loss may spread for a time and then become stable.

"In most patients," she went on as if by rote, "the retina recovers its function and a complete return of vision happens over a period of one to three years."

Hesitating, she finished as if she didn't want to remember the last part. "But in a small percentage of cases, sight is not recovered and eventually structural changes at the back of the eye take place. There is no known treatment for this condition."

"Excellent memory, Tory."

"I have a form of what's known as photographic recall," she agreed. "It's always been a lot easier to memorize and bring back the facts than it is to work with actual patients. If they just list their symptoms, I can diagnose and know how to begin treatment within a few seconds."

"I would've thought you'd be good with people," he told her as gently as possible. "You can be my doctor anytime." He had a feeling this might be a tender subject for her.

"I don't have enough patience to work well with adults. It's one of the reasons I'd hoped to work with kids," she admitted. "I'm always…jumping in…wanting to fix things. When what I should do is take my time."

Ben let that thought slide by unchallenged. There were a couple of times when rushing was exactly the right way to go, as he remembered. But then again, slow and steady had always been his favorite style. In most instances, that is.

Swearing softly under his breath, he fought the images of slowly peeling off Tory's clothing and easing himself into her waiting warmth. Damn it. Where was all this sexual hunger suddenly coming from?

He had made that vow of celibacy with the Brotherhood, and it'd been easy up until now to abide by the rules. The other members of the Brotherhood had been having their problems with the vow and at least one had decided to discard it.

Ben had so far refused to give in to any temptation. But being near Tory was sorely testing his resolve.

"So what are you going to do about your blindness?"

Her blatant jump right in made him laugh out loud. "You really aren't able to stay quiet, are you?" he asked past a choked rasp. "Are you always so pushy?"

"That's what my mother used to say. Her exact words were, 'stick your nose in other peoples' affairs often enough and you're apt to have it cut off.'"

"Well in my case, I don't mind the questions," he told her with another chuckle. "But the truth is there is nothing to be done except wait to see how bad this is going to get."

"But…"

He smiled at her, thinking how spectacular her cornsilk hair looked in the sunshine, and shook his head. "I'm coming to terms with it. There are lots of things worse than blindness in this world.

"The biggest problem is my practice," he went on. "Because my patients see me as a crystal gazer, losing my eyesight is the absolute worst possible outcome. It would be a sign of witchcraft to the elder traditionalists. They'll refuse to come anywhere near me for fear I might witch them, too."

For the first time since he'd known her, Tory sat quietly, lost in thought. He wasn't sure what was happening in that beautiful and smart head of hers. But he surprised himself by wanting to hold her hand while it happened.

He didn't touch her, though. That was just one step beyond what he thought was appropriate between doctor colleagues. Even ones that were fast becoming friends.

"I'll make you a deal," she finally said. "If I can get Dr. Hardeen to agree, I'll drive you around to see patients and work with you here in your clinic several days a week. At least until we can tell for sure whether your blindness will be permanent or not."

"Ray will be happy about the deal, don't worry about that. He wants my patients to continue receiving adequate medical treatment. What is *my* part of the bargain?"

"I want you to teach me the legends, the ceremonies and help me get a start on the language."

He nodded his head, delighted that she'd come up with it herself.

"But mostly I want to learn more about the plants. I am fascinated by all that stuff. Teach me what you know."

"Certainly," he agreed. "But there are others who know much more than I do. Perhaps…" He let the thought drop and held his breath.

Tory wondered why Ben had stopped talking in the middle of a sentence. He was staring off toward the back deck of his home with a startled look on his face.

Was his eyesight suddenly worsening? Or maybe it was going the other way. What a blessing that would be.

She turned her face to glance in the same direction as he did and was surprised to see an older woman coming toward them across the field. "Who's that?"

"I almost don't believe my own eyes. That's the medicine men's Plant Tender, Shirley Nez. I was just about to mention her to you, and there she is."

Tory got to her feet. "Well, I guess it must be Navajo magic. Mind over matter."

"Very funny," Ben grumbled as he, too, stood up. "Every culture has strange coincidences. Even an uptight one like yours."

Uptight? Was that what he thought of her? More to the point, was it true?

"Ya'aat'eeh," the older woman called out as she came near.

"Ya'aat'eeh," Ben answered with a nod. "I have someone I'd like for you to meet. Shirley Nez, this is—"

"The doctor known as Tory Sommer," Shirley broke in. "I'm glad to have the opportunity to meet you at last, Doctor."

"Please call me Tory. And the pleasure is mine, Shirley."

A nicely dressed woman in her early fifties, Shirley returned her smile.

"We were just speaking of this doctor's need to learn

the Navajo Way." Ben's face had turned down in a frown as he spoke to the older woman.

"If one wants to know the Way, there can be no mistakes on the journey," Shirley said, shaking her head at Tory. "Knowledge is a breathing thing that is meant to be shared. To try is a sign of wisdom, not of being out of balance."

"Have I offended you? I'm sorry, but I don't understand." Tory was beyond confused.

"Traditional Dine do not like to be called by their proper Anglo names," Ben told her. "It's disrespectful."

"Sadly, most of our young people ignore this tradition amongst themselves," Shirley said. "They have become modernized at schools. Since you see mostly modern Dine, there would be no way for you to have known."

Tory felt the smile spreading across her own face. She really liked this gray-haired lady in the navy pantsuit who had just gone out of her way to make the new kid on the block feel more comfortable.

"She's going to be helping me out here, and I've agreed to teach her some of the Way," Ben told Shirley. "But she's also very interested in the Plant Clan. I'd hoped that you would have the time to spend with her so she might learn about our neighbors and friends."

The Plant Clan? Tory resisted the urge to make a remark. She was beginning to accept that perhaps she should spend more of her time in keeping quiet and listening than in asking questions or jumping to conclusions.

She watched Shirley's eyes narrow as the woman seemed to be scrutinizing her. Reaching one hand out, Shirley lightly touched Tory's hair.

"Interesting. You are quite fair, and yet I sense that…" Shirley hesitated, dropped her hand and turned back to

Ben. "Yes. If she is willing to devote the effort, I will be happy to teach the lessons she needs."

"Thank you." Both Ben and Tory spoke at the same time.

"That's most generous, Plant Tender," Ben continued. "By the way, we have had an encounter this morning with an unusual raven."

Tory was startled by his quick change in the direction of the conversation, but decided it was still not smart to say anything. Something was sparking between the two Navajos. Something they obviously didn't want to share.

"Was it daylight?" Shirley asked him.

He nodded. "The sun was already over Beautiful Mountain, yes."

"Why don't you take a moment to call one of your *cousins* and tell them of your experience," Shirley said quietly. "I wish to speak to this young woman alone for a few minutes."

With another quick nod, Ben turned to Tory. "I'll be back shortly. You'll be safe out here with Shirley. She's very special to us, and one of the wisest people I've ever met. Listen to her with an open heart."

Safe? What a strange way for him to put it.

"Can you make it back inside by yourself?" Tory stopped him to ask about his eyesight, but she wasn't sure Shirley knew of his problem so she was caging her words.

"No sweat. I won't be gone long." With that, Ben turned and strode toward the house.

"His vision still comes and goes," Shirley said after Ben had disappeared into the house. "It makes it harder for him because he never knows what to expect at any time."

"He told you?"

"Yes. But his family and friends have no idea. Our young heart still hopes for a reprieve."

"Young heart?"

"Ben Wauneka belongs to a society of medicine men known only as the Brotherhood. They are all related in some way—most of them are clan cousins. Their group was formed for…uh…protection and informational purposes.

"The doctor is the true heart of the society," Shirley continued. "He seeks a return to the old ways. His desire is to put things in Dinetah back into harmony, not by force but by spirit. And he reminds us all of our heritage and our vows."

"Are things out of 'harmony' here?"

"It seems so. But it is not for you to worry about. When you hear of the Brotherhood, know that there is nothing for you to fear."

What a surprising thing for a nearly complete stranger to say. Tory was already feeling out of harmony herself.

Shirley took her hand. "Our 'heart' needs protection, and so far he has refused all offers. But it looks as if he has chosen you. I am pleased. You have a strong spirit and a curious mind. You'll be good for him."

"Ben needs protection? From what?"

Shaking her head, Shirley lifted a hand to brush back a strand of hair that had blown in her face. "That is not for me to say. But he could use a good friend and companion by his side through his journey of trials."

All of a sudden, Tory wanted nothing more than to be Ben's good friend. To help him through his upcoming months of vision problems and unsettled clinical practice. She wasn't sure why this woman's telling her she had a strong spirit made her so determined to prove it was true.

But strong spirit or not, Tory was still absolutely convinced that by the end of Ben's trials, her own heart would be wounded beyond the reach of any emotional first aid. Being doomed to pain didn't seem to make much of a difference to her, though.

"I have one more thing to say and then I will leave you two to work together." Shirley picked up Tory's other hand and turned them both palms up, staring down at them as she talked. "The Plant Clan is a critical part of the rituals and ceremonies of the medicine men. In fact without them, the Navajos' whole way of life would come to an end."

Shirley sighed and then looked into her eyes. "It is my calling to tend to the health of our friends the plants. I will teach you much more than how to plant and tend a garden. I will teach you to recognize each variety, know their uses and…where they are commonly found in Dinetah."

That last part seemed difficult for Shirley to say. Tory found herself asking a question, even though she had vowed to listen instead. "Is that especially hard to do? Learn where each kind grows the best?"

"Not hard. But it is a secret few people are allowed to share. The medicine men know. They must in order to perform their rituals. But the knowledge is sacred. Not many others have ever been allowed that privilege. It is passed down through the generations to only a chosen group."

"And you're going to tell me? But why? I'm not even Navajo." She pulled her hands to her sides.

"That is also not for me to say. But I have seen in your eyes that you will be a Plant Tender. You are one that the Plant Clan will respect and accept."

Shirley ended by declaring, "We will begin our studies in the next day or two."

Tory's mouth was hanging open again. Why did these people have to say the most amazing things when she was least expecting it?

"Excuse me," Ben called out as he walked across the lawn toward them. "I'm sorry to interrupt, but it seems I am needed at the Raven Wash gym."

"Has the school requested a curing ceremony to remove the *chindi?*" Shirley asked.

He nodded. "And no one else is available. The FBI just took away the police tape lines and the school would like to get back inside this evening so the basketball team can practice on their court."

"Wait a second," Tory blurted. "You lost me. *Chindi?*"

"If you'll agree to drive me down to the gym," Ben bargained, "I'll explain it to you on the way. I'd meant to ask you for a ride down to my SUV anyway. It's still parked in the school's lot."

"You can't drive," Tory told him.

"Yes," Shirley agreed. "It will be too dangerous for you to drive now that your vision goes more often."

Ben held his hands up, palms out in surrender. "I wasn't planning on driving. I'd hoped Tory would agree to take my SUV from now on. It's a lot safer vehicle to drive up in these cliffs than her old sedan."

Raising his eyebrows, he dropped his hands and smiled. "Is that okay with everyone?"

"Good. Good." Shirley smiled. "I must go now. I will be in contact with you both." With that last pronouncement, she turned and walked away.

Tory fought to get her voice back. "That is the most amazing woman," she managed at last. "Shirley just told me that I will become a Plant Tender like she is. I don't even know if I can grow living things or not, and now I'm going to be a Navajo Plant Tender. Do you think she was serious?"

"I've known Shirley Nez since I was born. She and my mother were cousins and good friends. And I have never heard her make a joke like that. If she says you will be a Plant Tender, count on it happening."

Chapter 7

Getting down the mountain in one piece and moving over to his SUV couldn't come too soon for Ben. Or for the sake of his poor backside. While Tory's old beat-up sedan bumped and wheezed along the rough shale, it was jarring both of their bodies beyond remedy.

As shaken as he felt physically, it didn't hold a candle to the earthquakes going on inside his brain. He'd tried hard to put the difficult things aside. But every time he had managed to think of anything else, his mind always came right back to a soft pair of gray-blue eyes.

"Are you okay?" he asked her between potholes.

"I will be when we get off this so-called road. Just try not to distract me in the meantime, please."

Okay, so he couldn't talk in order to keep himself occupied. And looking out the window was becoming problematic. He would see but a few of the familiar landscapes when all of a sudden his blind spot would grow and he ended up focusing on nothing but darkness.

Just then, the whispered notes of a baby's lullaby drifted through his subconscious the same way the warm spring breezes were gently blowing across his skin. The white woman doctor actually sang songs to plants. He hadn't heard anyone do that since his grandmother had been alive.

His thoughts went straight to the way Tory had jumped in front of him, using her own body to save him from a fall—several times now. She had listened intently to explanations of a culture that must seem like nonsense to someone who'd been raised in an Anglo world.

Most of all, she'd tried her damnedest to understand the Navajo philosophy and to find ways of being useful to him and to the Dine.

But absolutely none of those things were good enough reasons for a man to decide he was falling in love.

With a swift and silent curse, Ben chided himself. Love? Not him. And certainly not with a *bilagáana* woman.

Overpowering lust, that was all it was. He'd been having perfectly normal human responses as any male might to a very attractive woman. Not much more than could be expected from an enforced abstinence for the last three years.

But he would never allow himself to become involved with her beyond just lust and friendship. Loving an Anglo could very well be the ultimate disrespect to the memory of his traditional mother, who had been so steeped in Dine culture.

Once again, he tried focusing on the apricot glow from the sandstone cliffs of his homeland. And once again, his vision shifted in and out of focus.

He shook his head, but the memory of hearing Tory's story about becoming both mother and father to her brothers at such a tender age haunted him. There seemed no way of stopping the thoughts of how gray and sad her world must've been while his young life had been so full of love and color.

Yes, his lust was probably a normal function. But somehow, hearing her sing that lullaby to a plant had shaken his world.

All his plants looked perkier. The Brotherhood's mentor, Shirley Nez the Plant Tender, had actually smiled for the first time in many years. Ben was even beginning to hope that the *Yei* might yet intercede on his behalf and save his eyesight.

The whole thing pissed him off.

Hell. If he was really destined to lose his vision for good, he wanted the sight of soft gray-blue eyes and cornsilk blond hair to be the very last things he ever saw.

The mountains, ravines and canyons of Dinetah were already burned into his memory. They were a part of him, like the very nucleus of his cell structure.

He wanted the image of Tory to be that same way. A part of his memories for all time. Damn it.

Maybe he should give in to the lust. Let it wash over and consume him so the other deeper emotions connected to her would be pushed into the background of his mind.

Blurred sights and sharpened images of his beloved land passed by outside the sedan on the periphery of his vision. But he couldn't stop thinking of touching her— kissing her. He felt like a traitor to his beliefs.

A strange, feral noise suddenly broke into his reverie. And just that quickly, everything changed—again.

Danger. The Skinwalker war. The Brotherhood and what they stood for. All of it rushed back in through the open window with the shrill shriek of a large bird.

In one split second, Ben concluded he was actually grateful for the threat. He needed the distance and the reminder of what his life was really like.

"Tory, pull over."

"What? But there's no shoulder here. Can you wait a second until—"

"Pull over as close as possible to the cliff and stop. Now."

The tone in Ben's voice alerted her to the danger. Tory threw on the brakes, dragged the wheel to the left and ended up parked under the thick ledge of a granite shelf.

"Get out," he demanded as he shoved aside his seat belt. "Get out of the car."

If she'd had a moment to think, her unquestioning and quick response to his demands would've seemed odd. Not like her at all. But there was no time for thoughts as she jumped out of the car and dashed around to take his arm.

"Ben. Ben. I don't—"

"Let's go."

Instead of letting her help steady him, he grabbed her around the waist and turned them both in the direction of the sheer walls of the mountain beside the car. With sure and steady steps, he led her toward what might have been classified as a path, or maybe as a rough sort of stairs, that headed straight up the side of the cliff.

"Where are you taking me? And why?" she stammered.

"Up," he breathed with a hoarse rasp. "We're going up. Stay calm. I'll carry you."

"You'll do what? But why? How?"

Ben didn't seem able to waste the breath necessary to answer her. With his muscled arm still around her waist, he lifted her a few inches off the ground and began climbing. She gasped once, threw her arm around his neck and held on.

The slight edge of terror she'd felt when he'd spoken so sharply in the car overpowered her now with a vengeance. She closed her eyes and tried to keep her body from shaking itself right out of his arms.

Funny, but she trusted him implicitly. If Ben felt he could carry her upward through loose rocks and around shale spires without being able to see, then she would shut up and let him.

With her eyes closed, Tory's dream from last night blasted back into her conscious mind. *This* was her dream. Ben carrying her up the side of a rocky cliff away from danger.

She blinked open her eyes enough to see the side of his face as he tensed his jaw with the effort of carrying them both. He wore no war paint this time. And he had on a perfectly civilized long-sleeved cotton shirt instead of being naked from the waist up.

But he was wearing the same pale blue sash on his forehead as in her dream. He'd told her before they had left his home that it was part of the traditional medicine man's "uniform," along with the dark jeans and the silver-and-turquoise jewelry.

Now he was even whispering the same rhythmic chants as he had in her dream. This might just be the strangest thing that ever happened to her. Dream or no dream.

In a few minutes of his determined effort, the two of them finally reached a narrow plateau. He eased her down to her feet and then rushed them both back into a slight indentation in the sandstone slab that made a kind of shallow cave.

All the while, he never stopped the whispered chants. She could stand it no longer. "What's after us?"

"After us?" He stared down at her and she knew he was actually seeing her face this time. "Nothing. But…"

The ground beneath their feet began to roll, cutting off his words. Then a sudden rumble split the air around them. The noise became a deafening roar as small pebbles, then loose rocks and finally huge boulders rained down the sheer cliff past the safety of their indentation.

Tory buried her face against his chest. "Ohmigod."

The landslide lasted longer than he'd expected. Ben wasn't sure why the shriek of the bird had been the warning he had needed to really pay attention to the vibrations and get them out of the car. But he'd sensed the earth's movement and had known they would only be safe on higher ground.

When it was finally over, the dust from below rose up to surround their position with choking particles of shattered earth. He kept Tory's face tight against his chest with a hand at the back of her head. Burying his own face in her silky hair, he wrapped his arms around her to keep her close and safe.

This had been a Skinwalker attack. Those vibrations he'd noticed were the same ones he and the Brotherhood had come to recognize as a signal. He felt sure of it.

But the reason for the attack, and the fact that it had happened in broad daylight, were beyond his knowledge.

Was there some reason Tory had become a target? Or was it him they had wanted to destroy? Either way seemed strange, even for Skinwalkers.

He could be no real threat to them with the onset of his blindness. And Tory was not a Brotherhood warrior. In fact, she had few friends and no power in Dinetah—and certainly no allies.

Except for him.

At last, the cloud of dust particles settled and he eased slightly back from her. Just far enough to reach the cell phone in his pocket. He pressed the one button that would reach the Brotherhood and waited.

Not more than a second later, Kody Long answered his call. "Are you okay, cousin?"

"You know about the landslide?"

"Yes," Kody told him. "The Bird People informed us of the attack in progress. Michael Ayze is the closest to you. He should be at your position in a few minutes. I'm not far behind. Stay put."

As if they had any choice, Ben thought as he hung up the phone. His eyesight had gone dark again. And there was no way for him to know if showing themselves now might be exactly what the Skinwalkers were hoping for.

Were the evil ones lying in wait somewhere nearby? Or had the sacred chants he'd said worked to push them away?

Tory began to cough and lifted her forehead from his chest, but their bodies continued to touch. What was he going to tell her? It would be especially hard to think of something since he couldn't watch her expression as he made up a story. His cave of blindness was back in full force.

The violence of her coughing spasms tore at his emotions. He'd almost lost her, and he hadn't yet had the opportunity to memorize her face.

As gently as possible, he raised his hands and lifted her chin so she could breathe better. But the soft feel of her skin beneath his fingers made him hungry for more. Perhaps he could let his other senses make the memories for his eyes.

"You'll be okay," he whispered. "Stay calm and breathe through your mouth for a minute."

Using just the pads of his fingers, Ben touched her chin, forehead and the tip of her nose. He felt her go still beneath his tender strokes.

Other senses begged to join in the memory game. Cradling her face in both hands, he bent and let his sense of taste take a turn.

Her parted lips were every bit as soft and inviting as he'd been imagining. She tasted fresh and wild, like the earth of his home. And he fell into the miracle of her kiss.

As he stroked her lips and then eased his tongue inside her mouth, she started making tiny mewing sounds. Low, but urgent in the back of her throat.

That special scent of hers began to surround him with the wonders of her womanhood. She smelled of sage and something a little more spicy, like piñon tea—all earthy and robust and so alive it made him instantly hard.

His fingertips dropped to the long, silken length of her slender neck. Would she be flushing under his touch? As fair as she was, he'd be willing to bet on it.

But oh, how he wished to see it for himself. To watch her eyes glaze over as he found all the sensitive spots and pleasured her with both his touch and his kiss.

Running his forefinger down the valley between her breasts, he let his imagination fill in all the rounded curves and soft places he was dying to see. He popped the top button on her flannel work shirt and bent his head to let his lips and tongue follow his hands to places unseen.

Tory breathed out a sharp gasp and used her hands to push at his shoulders. "Ben, stop. Please stop. This isn't the time for…"

"*Ya'at'eeh,* my cousin. Where are you?" A deep male

voice, coming from right outside their hiding place, brought him out of the sensual stupor with a thud of reality.

Ben dropped his hands, leaned back and gave Tory a chance to straighten her clothes. Still not able to see anything, he was aware they were both covered in dust and had feared they might be buried under heavy rubble.

"Here, cousin." Ben called out to the voice he knew belonged to Michael Ayze. He was amazed at how fast the Brotherhood member had found them.

"Hang on to me," Tory said as she placed his hands on her shoulders. "Let me help you get out of here."

Ben's cousin, Michael Ayze, turned out to be a big guy. A burly fellow, with sensitive, intelligent eyes, he'd easily helped lift them both out of their slit in the rocks. Later, when they were back on solid ground, he'd told her he was a professor at Dine College and that he often participated in archaeological digs in the nearby areas. That was why he had located them so quickly.

They were safe, but she couldn't say as much for her car. It was buried under a ton of sandstone rocks and boulders. And according to the tribal police, it wouldn't ever be possible to put it back together.

Kody Long, another of Ben's cousins who'd introduced himself as a local FBI special agent, had offered to give them a lift down to Ben's SUV. As she and Ben rode in the high backseat of Kody's truck, Tory realized how different and smooth the ride felt in a vehicle meant for these rough conditions.

Ben—wonderful Ben—had not let go of her for one second since their rescue.

True, his eyesight had gone out again on the mountain

and hadn't come back. But Tory got the feeling that it was more than his just needing her eyes to lead him. He seemed to be okay with that detail.

No, this new closeness between them had come since the landslide and the kiss. It felt almost as if he was afraid of losing her, so he was determined to keep one hand on her at all times.

He shouldn't worry. She had no intention of losing sight of him, either. There hadn't been a moment to think of what might've happened had she not stopped the kiss— and why she'd thought to do that was also still a mystery. But she could not stand to think about it. Not yet.

"We're all grateful you two have survived the landslide," Kody told them as he carefully followed the road down.

"All?" she questioned. "Ben's family, you mean?" She couldn't imagine Kody was talking about the FBI.

Ben broke in. "Kody and I both belong to a society of medicine men, Tory. I'm sure Kody was talking about—"

"The Brotherhood, you mean? Well, that's nice they were worried about you. How do you suppose they heard about it so fast?"

Ben's expression said he'd just seen a ghost. Which, of course, was impossible since he wasn't seeing anything at the moment.

"How did you know about…"

"The Brotherhood? Shirley told me."

"Ah. What else did she say?"

"She said you were the heart of the group. The rest was all pretty hazy…but interesting."

"Ben called me for help from up on the cliff," Kody interrupted from the front driver's seat. "I'm the one with the big mouth. I called all of the Brotherhood to let them know about the trouble."

She thought about that for a moment. Pretty close relationship these men seemed to have. It made her a little curious to know why.

Before she could ask any more questions, Kody changed the subject to ask Ben one of his own. "While you're at the gym picking up your SUV, will you take the time to perform the Ghost Way ceremony for the principal? Are you well enough? I have to get right back to work. I'm hot on the trail of some information about the family of that teenager who died the other night."

"Perhaps," Ben answered quietly.

"The Ghost Way ceremony? Is that the one you and Shirley were talking about this morning? The one for getting rid of the *chindi*."

Ben laughed and tightened his grip around her shoulders. "You never forget anything, do you?"

"Not much, I'm afraid. And I still don't understand about the *chindi*."

She took a chance now that he was cornered and asked the other question that had been bothering her. "What's more, I don't really get the whole thing about medicine men ceremonies. You said it wasn't totally religious and yet not exactly just the alternative medicine, either."

Looking from Ben to Kody, she shook her head with their silence. "Can one of you please explain?"

Ben thought for a few seconds about what to say to her. He knew Kody would leave it up to him. But how was he to answer so she could easily relate?

"A big part of what it means to be Navajo is a sense of balance…harmony in all things, both natural and man-made," he began. "But bad stuff happens. And stressful happenings are difficult on any human being—even the Dine.

"With prolonged stress, you whites become mentally ill,

get stomach ulcers and contract psychosomatic sicknesses. The best way I can explain what the *hataalii* does is to relate it to Anglo psychiatric treatment. When the medicine man performs a 'healing' ceremony, the People believe the chants and potions will cure their problems. And so—they do."

"Ah. Mind over matter. The mind is a wondrous thing. That's very interesting."

"More than just interesting, Doctor," Ben told her with a scowl. "If you want to really make a difference to your traditional Dine patients, you must be able to relate to their needs. Talk their language and respect their beliefs."

He felt her put her hand over the one of his that had been resting on his knee.

"Yes, Doctor, I know that. And it's your job to teach me how. We have a deal."

Chapter 8

In a trick of nature more reminiscent of a magic show than something from real life, Ben's eyesight returned just as they pulled into the high school parking lot.

When Kody brought his truck to a stop near the gym, Ben reached for the door handle and jumped to the ground. "Let's go, Tory. I see Principal Billie heading this way. Someone must've seen us coming up the drive and let him know."

He turned to help her step down off the running board. She took his hand, but he knew she was quietly scrutinizing him and assuring herself that he could see.

"You gonna do the curing ceremony, cuz?" Kody hadn't shut off the engine and sat with his truck idling while he waited for a decision.

"Yes, I'm good. Thanks for the lift."

"No problem. You need any rides…or anything…just let us know."

Ben answered with a nod. Tory gave Kody a polite thanks and said how glad she was to meet him. And then his cousin roared off in a dusty cloud.

"This Brotherhood society must be really close," Tory began as she dropped his hand. "I don't think I've ever heard about a group of men being like that in the white world."

"Maybe not," Ben hedged. But he knew of certain squads of soldiers, both white and mixed race, who had become just as close—in times of war.

The secret war with the Skinwalkers, raging across his homeland, had made the Brotherhood what they were today. But he didn't feel comfortable discussing it with Tory. Not yet, at least.

Ben smiled down at her. "You have half the mountain stuck to your hair and clothes," he said in hopes of distracting her and changing the subject.

"I do?" She touched her hair. "You're just a little dusty, is all. Why did I get the worst of it?"

Reaching over to push a stray strand of her hair behind her ear, he lifted his eyebrows. "Maybe because you were protecting me and led the way out. I've been meaning to thank you for that."

She blushed and his whole body took notice of the rosy change in the color of her skin. "Don't be nuts." She laughed. "*You* were the one who saved us both by getting us up the side of that cliff. You were amazing."

He couldn't help himself. It was too late to hold back now that he'd touched her and his fingers knew the feel of her skin. He ran a finger down her jawline and lingered at the tip of her chin.

"You're the amazing one, Tory. Look at all the things you've already accomplished in your life. Getting through med school after starting from such meager circumstances, finding this way to pay off your student loans and settling in and meeting people in a place so far removed from everything you have ever known. You are one very special woman."

Embarrassed but secretly pleased, Tory shook her head. "That was nothing. It's my life. There isn't anything to do but live through it."

But none of it had prepared her for what she was dealing with now as he touched her face. The thought of their kiss, that life-altering and mind-twisting touch of his lips to hers, was distracting her beyond hope. She was stuck with this frustrating and unfulfilled urgency between them. A desperation for more stroking, touching and whatever else came next.

Making him stop had left her feeling as if she was holding on to her place on planet Earth by simply a sheer force of will.

"I'm glad you could make it, Doctor Wauneka." A middle-aged Navajo man Ben had pointed out as being the school principal called out from about ten feet away, finally breaking the hypnotic tension between them.

Ben waved him over. The salt-and-pepper-haired man in a blue suit walked up and shook his hand.

"We ran into a little trouble on the road or we would've been here sooner." Ben turned to her. "Dr. Tory Sommer, this is Earnest Billie. He's been the principal of Raven Wash High School for as long as I can remember."

On occasion, like when her brain had turned to mush from the gentle touch of a hard-as-steel Navajo doctor, Tory made a complete fool of herself. This was one of those terrible times.

"Ya'at'eeh," she said in what she hoped was a good im-

itation of the guttural sounds she'd been hearing whenever two natives greeted each other.

Both men stood stock-still and stared at her.

Principal Billie was the first one to recover. "*Ya'at'eeh,* Doctor Sommer. I had heard a new white doctor had come to our area to work at the Raven Wash Clinic. It's nice to meet you."

She knew her face was flushing bright red with embarrassment at the apparent mistake she'd just made. But she decided not to compound the error by apologizing. Not when that also might be something Navajo society didn't allow. Their customs were strange and confusing.

"My clothes are a mess," she mumbled as she tried desperately to dust her hands off on her slacks. "We were just in a landslide."

"Oh?" The principal turned to Ben for confirmation of what the obviously crazy white woman was saying.

"It wasn't anything," Ben told him. "But perhaps this doctor could be allowed to clean up in one of the school's restrooms while I perform your sing?"

"Yes, of course. I'll unlock the gym for you and then show her to the nurse's office. She'll be more comfortable there."

And someone would be around to keep an eye on the crazy woman doctor, Tory thought to herself. But she'd made enough mistakes for one day and kept her mouth firmly shut while she followed the two Navajo men over to the gym. Then she trudged on with the principal to the nurse's office.

Tory could tell Mr. Billie didn't much care for her. Without saying a word, he'd made it clear he felt she was out of place. Yet he was polite.

And she imagined that was a good lesson about most of the Navajo. One she would try to respect.

* * *

"April Henry. I can't believe it's you," Tory said when the principal had shut the door behind himself and left the two women alone. "What are you doing as the school nurse? Does Dr. Hardeen know you're holding down two jobs?"

April laughed and shrugged a shoulder. "He did when I was working here part-time. He was even the one who suggested the idea at first. But I don't have two jobs anymore. Not since I quit the clinic."

"You quit? But why?"

"Uh…" April looked embarrassed, but then she set her jaw and continued. "It was that horrible Russel Beyal. Dr. Hardeen put him in charge of the entire afternoon shift."

April shivered in the heat of non-air-conditioned midday as if the very thought of the man unnerved her. "There is something beyond spooky about that guy. No way was I going to put up with him being my permanent supervisor. He studies women like a hawk getting ready for a meal. Ugh."

"Well, maybe you're right about Russel. But the clinic is sure going to miss you."

April brightened. "Thanks, Doc. I'll miss everyone there, too. But this is better for me. My fiancé is the head coach here and I'll get lots of vacations when the school-kids do. We're going to be married this summer so the loss of half my income won't be too bad."

The nurse did a double take and shot a glance up and down Tory's body. "What happened to you? You look like you fell in a Dumpster."

Laughing at her own expense, Tory explained and asked for a place to clean up. She was hoping the bathroom would not have a mirror so she wouldn't have to face her filthy image, but no such luck.

Simply awful. For a split second she found herself grateful that Ben's eyesight had been growing worse.

What a horrible thing to even think. She chastised herself, but a tiny niggle of guilt remained.

There wasn't much she could do to fix up the way she looked. She needed a bath, and her clothes just might have to be burned in the end. Taking off her shirt and pants, she shook them out the best she could. Then she washed her face and hands and combed her fingers through her hair.

The whole time, she was wishing for a leprechaun or fairy with a magic wand to come along and make her look beautiful so Ben wouldn't have to see her like this again. Sighing with resignation, she put her clothes back on and reentered April's office.

"How long do you think Ben's curing ceremony will take?" she asked.

"I don't have a clue. Sometimes those medicine man ceremonies take days."

When Tory's mouth dropped open, April quickly added, "Oh, but I'm sure Dr. Wauneka's ceremony will be a lot shorter. Maybe a couple of hours?"

"Could you tell me what this *chindi* thing is all about?" Tory was concerned that it would be some superstitious ritual she really didn't want Ben to explain.

"Yeah, I asked an uncle to teach me about the *chindi* once. I was curious, too. I mean, I went to nursing school off the reservation and this prohibition about not entering a building where a person died for four days afterward seemed pretty far out there to me."

"Is that true? Four days. Just because someone passed away in the place?"

"My uncle is an professor of anthropology at Arizona

State. He's done studies of the native Southwestern Indians' ancient beliefs. Mostly the Hopi, Navajo, Pueblo and Apache.

"He told me the Dine have been a highly advanced people for many hundreds, if not a thousand years. Our *ancient ones* were aware of the effects of bacteria and viruses long before they knew what those things were. And they apparently observed that contagion could be spread by the newly dead."

April blinked her eyes at Tory and continued. "To warn the People to stay away, they called that danger *chindi,* which was already the word for the evil spirit that resides in all of us. The elders taught the people to avoid the dead and the place of death for at least four days so the evil would have a chance to go away—even longer if it was in a closed place where the *chindi* might be caught."

"I see. That's actually very clever. Probably saved the Dine from dying off in a plague like the Europeans did several times in their history. So what does the curing ceremony do?"

"In modern times, doctors know pretty quickly when a place is contagious and should be decontaminated. So now, mostly to please the elders I think, if the death was an accident or a heart attack or something, the medicine man can use one of his chants and curing ceremonies to clear the air and make it all right to go in again."

The idea of mind over matter gave Tory another idea. "April, do you know of a curing ceremony for blindness?"

"No. Why? You're not having trouble with your eyesight, are you?"

"Just curious." Tory didn't want to field any more questions on the subject. She'd already said too much.

She had considered asking April for a ride home. Her

house wasn't that far. But she didn't want to leave in case Ben needed her.

"I should let you get back to work," she told April. "By any chance is there an online computer that I could use to do a little research?"

"In the library. But we'll have to clear it with the librarian. And I know some Web sites are blocked so you won't be able to get access to those places."

"No problem," Tory said with a chuckle. "I doubt there'll be a block on medical-school libraries. Thanks."

She might just shoot off a couple of e-mails, too. If it would be allowed.

Tory's frustration was growing by the minute. There had to be some way to help Ben besides just driving him around and helping out with his practice. If there was, she was determined to find it.

Ben stuck his head into the school nurse's office and looked around. The place seemed empty. He was grateful that his vision was still good after a long couple of hours doing the curing ceremony.

But now, when he was really dying for a glimpse of Tory, she was nowhere in sight.

He turned to leave, but then caught the sound of someone whispering coming from a back room. Curious, he quietly walked over to the partially closed door and listened.

Hearing Tory's voice speaking softly, he leaned in and decided to eavesdrop for a few moments before he interrupted and barged right in. After a second, he realized she was talking to one of the school's students, a girl who must've come to the nurse's office because she'd felt ill.

"Thanks for helping me out in the library, Dr. Sommer,"

he heard the young female voice say. "I don't know what happened to make me just pass out like that."

Ben listened as Tory quietly asked the girl about her eating habits and then about the possibility she might be pregnant. Tory had a firm but pleasing bedside manner, he was happy to note. She'd been mistaken when she'd claimed she had trouble dealing with patients.

"No, it's nothing like any of that," the girl said. "My boyfriend…well, he says it's wrong to have sex before marriage. And besides that…" The girl's voice suddenly lowered even more than before and she began to use a conspiratorial whisper. "It's not allowed by the members of a new society he's just joined. They claim it's bad for the health and will ruin your athletic ability."

New society? Ben's curiosity took a more sober turn.

"Your boyfriend is on an athletic team?" Tory asked casually.

"He's a wrestler. State Junior Division champ. I'm on the girls' basketball team, too."

"Oh? Did your boyfriend know the wrestler that died the other night?"

"We both did. He was…he was a member of the society. But oh, Dr. Sommer, you're not allowed to know about the society. I shouldn't have said anything. My boyfriend will kill me if he finds out I told."

To Tory's credit, she stayed calm and kept her voice low and easy. "I won't say anything. But I really think you should come into the Raven Wash Clinic tomorrow so I can run a few tests to see why you fainted."

"I can't."

"Won't your parents let you see a white doctor?"

"No, nothing like that. They're cool. It's that new society's rules They say *all* doctors are bad.

"You see, the guys that belong all take this powder stuff," the girl continued. "To make them stronger. My boyfriend thinks it's steroids and that's why they're not allowed to even *talk* to any doctors. For fear someone will find out and make them stop."

"If it is steroids, then I agree," Tory told her. "They should stop. In fact, if they don't know what they're taking, they shouldn't be taking it. It could be really dangerous. But what does any of that have to do with you?"

Ben couldn't hear the girl's answer, but he heard Tory's voice getting slightly more shrill. As if she was concerned but couldn't make the girl understand her fears.

The sound of footsteps told him someone was heading for the door he'd been standing behind. He moved away and went back outside the nurse's office, counted to ten and then reentered as if he'd just arrived.

"Ben," Tory said when she caught sight of him and closed the door to the other room behind her. "Is the ceremony over? I'm glad to see you. Can you still see me now?"

"Yes to everything. Are you ready to go?" He wanted to talk to her about what he'd overheard. But not here.

Before they left the high school, Tory sought out April, told her about the girl still lying on the cot in her office and then asked the nurse to surreptitiously find out the name of the girl's boyfriend. Ben had quietly mentioned he'd overheard the bulk of the conversation. But the two of them decided to wait until they were alone to discuss it.

She climbed into the driver's seat of his SUV and waited for him to buckle up. "Where to?"

"I doubt that the Department of Highways has had a

chance to clear out the road to my house. So, if we want to clean up and rest, we'll have to go to yours."

Tory hadn't thought about the highway being blocked. "You mean there isn't any other way up there? How long will you be kept out of your place?"

Ben smiled and shrugged. "There is another way in, but it's about a three-hour-extra drive. I imagine the road should be cleared by tomorrow. So not much need to waste the time going around…unless you don't want to invite me to your home for tonight."

The mere thought of being alone with him—anywhere—suddenly brought back the cloud of lust she'd been trying to shake. Oh, Mother Mary. She was obsessing about a man. How could she?

Looking up into his dark brown eyes, she wondered, *how could she not?*

"Of course you're invited to my house." She started up the SUV. "We'll be there in a few minutes."

In the ten minutes of their drive home, Tory thought of nothing but the way his hands on her face had felt so intimate. So awe-inspiring. He had blown her away with just his fingertips and his lips.

Dear God, she had to do something to help him get past this eye disease. He'd given her the gift of caring and intimacy. Though she knew better than to expect anything more, she just had to return the favor.

In the meantime, she would figure out how to stop all these sexual stirrings. She would. They were obviously not ever going to become a couple—the word couple as applied to the two of them was almost laughable. It might even be considered a joke, if it didn't hurt so much to know the time was coming when she would never see him again.

As they walked into her house, Ben quickly went from one room to the next. He told her he was trying to memorize the layout and the steps necessary to get around in case his eyesight went back out suddenly.

After making sure he was okay, she excused herself and took a shower. She needed to clean up. But as the hot water sluiced over her body, the sizzling tingles against her thighs and the heady smell of her soap turned her thoughts right back to that sensual moment between the two of them up on the mountain.

This was an impossible situation. She couldn't concentrate on anything but the dream of his hands on her body. What could she do to put an end to all these cravings so she could get down to what was important?

There were so many new things for her brain to consider instead of sexual longings. She needed to talk to Dr. Hardeen about taking a few days off to work with Ben every week. She wanted to get out in the garden with Shirley as soon as possible and learn about the Plant Clan. And now she was very concerned about the idea of some sort of cult pushing the use of steroids and taking over at the high school.

But still, behind all those thoughts, the memory of the erotic delight in Ben's touch kept interfering. Damn her screwy hormones, anyway.

After drying off and putting on clean clothes, Tory sucked up her resolve and went out to the kitchen to find Ben—and came to a roaring halt when she found the man, minus his shirt, cooking something on her stove.

"I…" Nope, the voice sounded too rough.

She cleared her throat and tried again. "I didn't think I had anything fit to eat in the place. I've been trying to get to the grocery store."

Yeah. That sounded cool enough.

Then he turned his head, and her knees buckled. She was forced to grab hold of a kitchen chair in order to stay upright.

"You look…clean," he said with a smile in his voice.

But the desire in his eyes was much more graphic. The sensual need and something else that resembled desperation was as plain on his face as a pornographic film. She couldn't speak.

"I hope you don't mind," he said as he turned back to the stove. "I foraged around in your cabinets and went out to the garden. We're having spaghetti primavera. I assume you'll like the way I make it."

"I'm sure I will." Whatever he did was okay by her, and now that he wasn't looking directly at her, she was getting her footing again.

"After we eat, I'll help you take a bath if you want to clean up."

Had she really just said that? What an idiot.

He flipped her a look that said he certainly would like to clean up in the bathtub—with her. "Thanks. Don't look so horrified—I knew what you meant, Doctor. It's my clothes I'm most worried about, though. Can you stuff them into the washer with yours and find me a blanket or something to wear until they're clean?"

"Uh…I don't have a washer. But I'll take them down to the laundromat after dinner. It won't take too long."

"I don't think it's a good idea for you to be out on the roads after dark."

"Oh, for heaven's sake. Don't you people ever give that a rest?" She took a deep breath and counted to ten. "It will still be light after dinner. It's early yet. I'll be back well before dark. I promise."

Ben nodded sharply. "Okay, then. Maybe when you get back we can try that bathtub deal. It sounds like fun."

Chapter 9

"Ben? Where are you?"

The house seemed too still. She noticed a light in the kitchen but the rest of the house was cast in darkness. Tory worried that something terrible had happened to him.

She set the basket of clean clothes down and went searching, switching on overheads along the way. Finding a light on in the bathroom and a wet towel over the bar but Ben nowhere to be seen, she continued down the hall and pushed the door open to check her bedroom.

Through the shadows being thrown into the room by the lighted glow from the hallway, she saw him sitting cross-legged on her bed with the blanket loosely over his shoulders. Thank God.

"You didn't answer me," she said. "What's going on?"

"It's already dark. You promised. I've been concerned."

It was more than that. She knew by the way he was

sitting there and staring blankly at the wall that he was blind again.

"It's only just past dusk. But I'm sorry if you were worried." She moved to the bed and sat beside him.

Reaching over to push a strand of wet hair off his face, she was truly mad at herself for not having been here to help him get around. To be his eyes.

But when he flinched away from the touch, everything changed for her.

"Ben. Please." The hum of desire that arched between them was too much for her to ignore any longer.

She took his hand and placed it against her breast. "Forgive me for not being here when you needed me. But right now, I need you. Don't turn away. Please...please make love to me."

He stilled. But he didn't pull his hand away.

"I can't need you," he whispered. "I can't let myself."

"Why? Because you're afraid of being too dependent on my help? Don't lose hope that way. There's a chance your blindness won't become permanent."

"No, it isn't that." He voice sounded strangled, as if it cost him dearly to speak.

"Then what?"

For one long moment, she held her breath and waited to find out her fate. She knew he'd made some kind of deal with himself where she was concerned. She'd seen his hunger, could feel his desperation. But she had also seen that he'd been holding back—perhaps out of some sense of honor.

Now would he accept what she was offering? She wished with everything in her that he could look at her and really see her. See her need.

Finally, he spoke. "I have responsibilities that you don't understand."

He was right: she didn't have any idea what that meant. But his hand remained under hers and against her breast. He hadn't pulled away.

Even in the shadows of the room, she could see his nostrils flare as he licked his lips. He might not be able to see her need, but she saw his. And knew he had to be feeling her heart fluttering under his fingers. It was beating so frantically, she was half afraid the darn thing might jump right out of her chest.

Ben wanted what she wanted. She could smell it emanating from his every pore. The pheromones wafting around the room had to be so thick she was surprised they were both still able to breathe.

She had never *ever* wanted anyone like this. It was insane, and she was becoming giddy from the crazy sensations streaming along just under her skin.

Sliding her other hand under his, she began to unbutton her blouse. Slowly, praying he would stay with her, she sandwiched his hand with both of her own and slipped all the buttons free.

Letting the blouse fall open to reveal her bare breasts, she heard his slight intake of breath when he realized she didn't have a bra on. Thank heaven she hadn't had the time to do laundry all week.

What she decided to do next might've been too huge a risk to take, considering how conflicted he was about her. But she held her breath anyway and reached for his other hand.

Tory just had to feel his hands on her, and was dying to touch him in return. She'd dreamed of it, craved it, secretly prayed for it since the night they'd first met.

Now that she had him in her bed, she wasn't about to give up without knowing—knowing him.

He passively sat there while she took both of his hands

and placed them on her naked breasts. For just a second, she reveled in the warm feel of his rough palms against her tender nipples. She ached for him.

Slowly, steadily, she began to rub his hands across her chest, letting both of them get used to the sensual sensations of skin on skin. God, how she wished he could see how her breasts peaked and tightened under his touch. He wouldn't be able to resist. Just as she found it impossible to resist any of this herself.

Their joining had to happen. She wouldn't be able to go on breathing if they didn't make love to each other tonight.

Her body began to shake, trembling, nearly drowning her with need. Being this close, hearing the air going in and out of his lungs and smelling his masculine scent was becoming exquisite torture.

"Ben, please," she whimpered. "Touch me. Taste me. Let me touch you." She knew she sounded desperate.

A keening moan, so low and sad it broke her heart, came from the depths of his gut. Whatever demons had been controlling him must've taken flight in that groan.

He shrugged off his blanket and pushed at the material of her blouse, still clinging to her shoulders. With a war cry sounding both savage and feral, he ripped the seams and tore it from her body. Then, tumbling her backward on the bed, he pinned her below him.

"Yes," she cried. Dizzy with relief, she was nearly blinded by the desire between them. "Ben, oh, yes."

Lost. When Ben covered her mouth with his own, demanding, soothing, nipping, laving, he was done for.

From some distant place, he had heard the sound of his name coming from her lips and felt more turned on than he had ever been. It wasn't just the enforced abstinence;

it was her. Tory. With that breathless, out-of-control voice that seeped right inside him.

She tasted like clouds, all soft and wispy. Just like the angel he'd dreamed she would be. But it also seemed to him she was light enough that if he lifted his head, she might drift away on a breeze.

So he didn't. He kept on kissing her and kissing her, lingering, tasting, testing. Until a dizzy fire built in his brain.

Wiggling under him, she dug her fingers into his shoulders. He didn't dare let her move away. And he was guessing she wanted this to go further, the same way he did.

In a lightning move that surprised even him, he grabbed her wrists and raised them above her head with one hand so he could stretch her body out. Then with the other hand, he let his fingertips see all the hidden places that his eyes could not.

Bending his head to take one of her taut nipples into his mouth, he let his free hand roll the other peak between thumb and forefinger. Every sense was on high alert, taking up the slack where his vision had failed.

Hearing her moans, smelling her slight scent of citrus mixed with musk, tasting the salty brine of the sweat on her skin. His head was filled with heady, breathtaking sensations.

She called out to him. Whimpered. Begged. Cooed. And finally screamed.

Sliding down her body, he dragged his mouth over her flesh. His blood thickened, boiled. She grabbed handfuls of his hair, holding his head to her body and begging to be released from the tension he knew coiled inside her.

He began to hum—low and soothing, as his lips whispered along her skin. Wanting more time to stir and cherish—more time to please them both—he did the opposite of what she wanted and slowed down.

Ben's mind went back to long ago. To a time when his mother's words hadn't made much sense. But now they did.

"Sex is a sacred sharing, my son," she'd told him. "It's the way your spirit and the spirit of your beloved can dance together in the flesh."

Without being able to see Tory's reactions, he clearly felt their spirits mingling, soaring, rising up together. It was like nothing in his experience.

Her body was so solid and sleek. He cherished her—with fingers, tongue, and most of all with his heart. When he nudged through the tightly wound curls to the mound at the apex of her thighs, his imagination went wild. He just knew the hair there would be as blond as on her head. And he suffered greatly from the lack of being able to see for himself.

She cried out as he touched his tongue to her hidden nub, and he felt her spinning out of control. But one spin wasn't enough. Not nearly enough.

His actions had to tell her everything he would never have the words to say.

He sat up and brought her up with him—touching her everywhere—with hands frantic to learn every inch in the short time they would be together like this.

She laughed at his frenetic pace. Then she shrieked. And finally she growled, shoving at his shoulders to make him lie back so she could take charge.

This position made him more vulnerable, especially since he couldn't see. But he wanted her to know he trusted her—just for tonight.

Tory could hardly bear the tension building to unbelievable heights inside her body. But as she lay her hands against Ben's chest and felt his heart thundering under her palms, she vowed to stay with him.

Now. Tonight. Forever. Or for however long he wanted her.

His smell wrapped around her senses. Never before had she felt the heat of a man's breath or the touch of his tongue in the golden place between her thighs. She hadn't even been able to imagine it.

But now she would never forget. Never.

Payback time, she thought smugly.

Leaning over, she kissed his erection and ran her tongue over the smooth, silky edges of him. She wanted to hear him beg as she had, wanted to give him back a tiny amount of the pleasure he had given her.

She listened as his breathing changed, became shallow and rough. But as she laved and explored his body, the heat in her own core grew beyond her ability to hold back.

A momentary panic about protection reminded her of the condoms she'd stashed in her bedside drawer. At the time it had seemed way out of character for her to even think of such a thing. But now, all she could do was be grateful.

In seconds she had one out of the package and fitted down over him. Then straddling his body, she eased herself lower and took him into the place that had somehow known that their joining this way would feel like coming home.

The shock of how right they were together took her a minute to get used to. She gasped and stilled.

And then Ben laughed, growing even harder inside her. His laugh was such a carefree, passion-filled sound that her heart warmed and turned gooey.

Displaced, she felt adrift—forever taken by his spirit, even knowing full well this was likely to be their only time together.

Wrapping herself around him, she let him fill her, going farther, deeper. As deep as he could go. Deep enough to touch her lost heart.

She shoved the hopeless yearning for a lifetime of his touch aside for now, and just experienced the shattering feeling of fusing body to body, mind to mind.

Just when she thought they were both about to go over the edge, he stilled inside her. "Let me touch your face," he groaned in a hoarse voice. "Let me feel what my eyes cannot see. I have to know that this affects you the way it is affecting me. Let me. I beg you."

Chills and fever ran along her spine simultaneously, capturing her in a field of electricity. She would give him anything. Always.

She lifted his hands and, with the most gentle of touches, placed his fingertips against her face. He ran them lightly around her eyelids, over her forehead, and finally stroked her lips.

Opening her mouth, she took his forefinger inside. Then slowly she began to move her lower body against his. As their thrusts grew harder, faster, she mimicked the movements with her mouth, sucking and pulling on his finger as her internal muscles sucked and pulled him deeper to her core.

The power of it overcame her, temporarily driving her blind with sensations she could scarcely believe.

Too soon the lights exploded in her head. At the same time she heard him shattering, too, crying out with the same shocked gasp of surprise. She collapsed down against his chest and wondered how his racing heart could be standing such a strain.

She reached for his face, wanting to let him know without words that she was still with him. But when she found tears clinging to his cheeks, her own eyes welled up.

The majesty and power of their passion had affected him as much as it had her.

But Tory never cried. Not even when her father had died and she'd been forced to become the parent to her brothers. And she refused to allow herself the luxury of feeling anything so deeply about Ben, either. Not now.

Yes, she loved him. Unreasonably, because they were not meant for each other in the long haul. But she would not deal with the pain of losing him now. Perhaps later, when the nights were long, cold and lonely, she would take out her pain and face it squarely.

This was a moment all for pleasure. So she closed her eyes, wrapped her arms around him and quietly listened as his breathing leveled out and she knew he'd fallen asleep.

It was a small, whimpering moan that woke him. Out of force of habit, Ben opened his eyes and discovered he could actually see in the dim light before dawn.

The minute he looked around, he knew he wasn't home. That was when the soft, warm body next to his flexed slightly and threw an arm over his chest.

Instantly hard again for the third or maybe that was the fourth time, he let all his senses revel in her nearness. *Tory.* The word itself captured his attention.

Her musky, special scent had become familiar enough to him now that he would never get it out of his system. His fingertips might never forget the silky feeling of her skin. And his tongue…

The taste of her, of all her secret places, would be with him always. The satiny, salty place on the underside of her breast would come back to haunt him whenever he least expected it. And the feel of the smooth spot on the inside of her thigh, trembling under his tongue's assault, would be there every time he closed his eyes and licked his lips.

How could he have made such a huge mistake?

He'd had no idea it would be like this. So powerful and…unforgettable.

He remembered thinking when they'd first met that somehow they were meant to be. But he'd chalked that up to typical Navajo romanticism. And he'd hoped that giving in to her sensual pull, even against his Brotherhood vows, would rid him of such poetic notions.

No such easy ways out for him. But their being together like this—for always and ever—was an impossibility.

Why the hell hadn't this all-consuming sort of thing happened with a Dine woman? Tory was so…not Navajo.

Ben had years ago dedicated his life to respecting his mother's traditionalist views, despite the fact that he refused to give up being a modern physician and helping the Dine in more ways than one. He'd promised in his mother's memory to find a way to straddle both worlds— for the good of the Navajo Nation.

But falling in love with a *bilagáana* woman… His mother would never have understood. Never. He didn't understand it himself.

Tory moved against him once more and murmured what sounded like a sad sob. His hand automatically went to her hair, to soothe and protect.

He wanted her again so badly right now that he found himself covered in sweat from the effort of holding back. She was so sweet—hot and sweet. Bold, wild, tender, demanding. Just the thought of hearing her laugh—and scream—was driving him crazy with the need to hear it again.

It would be so easy. So right. To slip back inside her and let her smooth warmth take away his regrets.

But he couldn't do such a thing to her. It was a bad feeling knowing he still needed to use her friendship until his eyesight either returned for good—or didn't.

Then, either way, it was clear he would have to do without her when she left the rez to continue her career.

That was an indisputable fact and hard enough to deal with. How could he hope to explain to such a friend why they couldn't be more in the meantime? Not when the rightness of it was so obvious to both of them.

No way. He would just lay here quietly, looking at her and holding her until daylight. He could do that, right?

Maybe *he* could. But his senses refused.

The pads of his fingertips began to insist on feeling her nipples pucker under their touch. His ears were demanding to hear more of her soft sighs as they came together.

Tory lifted her lids sleepily, looked up at him and smiled. "You can see again, can't you?"

"Hmm."

Stretching herself along the length of him, she yawned. "Then would you do me a favor?"

"Okay."

She slid her hand down his chest, and lower still. "Make love to me again. But this time I want you to see us. I want you to watch what you do to me."

And just that fast…all his vows were forgotten.

What exactly was she supposed to say to Ben when he came back from the yard through the kitchen door?

What did you say to a man who had spent the night igniting your entire body with one touch, or with one smoldering sigh?

Did one say, "Excuse me, but please don't touch me again because I'll explode if you do?" Or maybe, "Can't you just go blind again, so I won't have to face you while you stare at me with that intense look you get?"

Not damned likely.

Especially not since he had left her in bed without so much as a word this morning. She had wanted more time to curl against him. More time to smooth her hands over his body, even though she was quite sure that last night had been the one and only time they would ever come together like that.

But she'd awoken alone and then panicked. Jumping out of bed, she had grabbed an old robe and raced through the house looking for him. Was he blind again and in trouble?

Then she'd spotted him. Outside the back door in just his jeans, facing the rising sun and chanting his prayers. She took her first breath since waking up.

Putting on a pot of coffee, Tory tried not to think of what they had done together during the night. It was too fresh a memory and too intense.

She had to find a way to talk to him civilly. Without begging for more times like last night. They had to work out some sort of tentative working arrangement. She had promised to help him. And she would never back down on anything she'd told him. Not him.

He stepped back into the kitchen then, and she lost the power of speech. Fine. She wouldn't say a word to the man she'd come to love in a way that was probably obsessive.

Ben took a breath and smelled the coffee. His body was

tight, fit, strong. He'd expected to be weakened by having sex—wasn't *that* why the ancient warriors had abstained just before a battle?

But he wasn't weak. Far from it. He felt energized and ready for a fight.

And that fact made him madder than hell.

What about the Brotherhood vows of celibacy? They had been his damned idea in the first place. Maybe Kody and Hunter had been right all along. Sex didn't seem like such a bad thing for his energy after all.

But then he spotted Tory and all his irritation came back with a bang. Why had he let her get to him like that?

He needed her to be his eyes. Why had he taken the chance of ruining their relationship for one night of pleasure? Stupid. Stupid.

"You want a shower before we leave?" she asked without turning to look at him.

Tory wasn't sure how she could stand to see him watching her again right now.

"I'm not going with you to the clinic today. One of the Brotherhood men will pick me up from here."

"Oh? Well then, can we talk about what we learned yesterday from that young girl at the high school before I have to leave for work? We haven't had a chance—"

"No," he said sharply. "Don't stick your nose in where it doesn't belong, Tory. Remember what your mother told you."

She spun around to glare at him, refusing to believe her ears. To go from a night of soft sighs and whispered endearments to this?

"Why not?" she demanded. "I asked April to find out the name of the girl's boyfriend. Maybe we could talk to him, see if the powder really is steroids."

"Stay out of it."

Suddenly unreasonably angry, Tory's mind filled with questions. That so-called *society* the girl had mentioned couldn't possibly be connected to the Brotherhood. Could it?

Shaken up with mixed emotions, all she could manage was, "Fine."

"Fine," he snapped in return.

But in the back of her mind, she was almost positive the two societies could not be connected. Shirley Nez seemed too honest and solid to ever be associated with something like that. And after another thought, neither could Ben.

She took a breath and started again. "Are you mad at me?"

"No." His voice dropped lower and grew hoarse. "I just shouldn't have let last night happen. It can't happen again, Tory."

"I know." But she felt there was something else he wasn't telling her. "Did I embarrass you yesterday with Principal Billie?"

He swung his chin in her direction and stared out of gorgeous deep brown eyes that she knew were actually registering her image. "What? When?"

"When I greeted him in Navajo."

Ben's eyes softened and crinkled around the edges. "Not at all. Far from it. It was just such a surprise to hear an excellently inflected Navajo word coming out of the mouth of…someone who looks like you. It stopped me for a second."

He turned, looked out the window, and she saw him smiling to himself. She was profoundly grateful for the break in the tension of having him watch her so intently.

"You are very bright, Tory," he said without turning. "Almost too street-smart for your own good. Please be careful here in Dinetah.

"Do you have a cell phone?" he added, and surprised her by the sudden change.

"No. I can't afford one on my salary at the clinic. Why do you ask?"

"I'll have one delivered to you at the clinic later today," he said without answering her question. "It'll be preprogrammed for one-touch dialing. If you ever feel afraid, or even get a little nervous feeling—use it."

"Will it be connected to 911? The police?"

"No, to the Brotherhood. One of us will always be nearby and can reach you much faster than the police."

Okay. The world just tilted out of balance again. What in God's name was she to do about him?

Chapter 10

The shadow known within the Skinwalkers as the Raven was now in his human form. Picking up the special satellite phone, he held it to his ear. "Yes?"

"I understand yesterday's landslide caused some chaos for the Brotherhood. Nice work." The Raven's boss, the Navajo Wolf, sounded pleased, but still his voice carried restrained control.

"Enough of a distraction," the Raven began, "to keep Dr. Wauneka out of his office for a few days at least. And I believe the white woman doctor will continue to disrupt and distract him, as well. Keep him from following up with our young recruits at the high school."

"Yesterday's result is better than you know," the Wolf told him. "So many of the enemy stayed occupied for most of the afternoon that it allowed me the time to meet with a representative of one of the pharmaceutical companies."

"Did he accept our research stats? Do they seem to be buying into the idea that we've uncovered an ancient cure for lung cancer?"

The Wolf chuckled so low and deep it sounded like a growl of pleasure. "Of course. It's another fine phony research job of yours, along with the help of my excellent mind control. But…"

"Yes?" The Raven found himself holding his breath. *But* was not a word he liked to hear from a man as dangerously on the edge as his boss.

He'd personally seen the Navajo Wolf rip a man's arm from his body for simply making a bad joke in his presence. And he'd heard of much worse things being done by the one who had promised to make them all wealthy beyond their wildest imaginings.

"There's something else you can do for the cause, Raven. That one plant you cited as part of the supposed studies, the *Aralia racemosa*…"

"Elk Clover or Leaf Scar, we call it. What about it?"

"I'm concerned someone will recognize the fact that we are removing all traces of that plant from its normal habitat in Navajoland."

"No one but a few old medicine men and Plant Tenders ever go near where it grows. And the *hataaliis* aren't there to gather that particular thing. They go to those areas for other sacred plants for use in their ceremonies."

"Still. Someone might notice and wonder why. We cannot have anyone asking questions like that. At least not until it's too late to do anything about it."

"When the drug company's lab studies its properties, we know they will find what we want them to find," the Raven said in as soothing a tone as possible. "That it increases interferon synthesis in infected white blood cells.

They'll have to accept the hypothesis for the rest of our formula and give us that multimillion-dollar grant for more studies."

The Raven stopped and took a breath. "None of the old Dine medicine men can do anything to ruin our plans."

The Navajo Wolf cleared his throat menacingly. "Send a few of the new young men recruits out to those remote areas to stand watch in shifts. Have them threaten or kill anyone who comes around. Make whatever they do look like witch magic so everyone else will stay away."

The Raven sighed quietly, but agreed. In his opinion, there were other far more important things to take care of. He'd already carved too much time out from his regular job in order to complete his Skinwalker duties, and he needed to get back to work. Another problem, finding new methods for slowing down the Brotherhood, was also becoming increasingly critical.

And not the least in importance was making the time to study why the Skinwalker leaders had all begun to show unusual physical signs of stress after several changeovers into their animal personas. But he would keep that one to himself for a while longer.

No, for now he would do his best to accomplish whatever the Wolf wanted. The Raven was rather fond of his life, and intended to keep breathing as long as possible.

Exhausted after a little over half a day's work at the clinic, Tory popped some change into the drink machine in the break room and searched the selections for something cold that also had lots of sugar and caffeine.

She needed all the extra reserves of energy available. Which was dumb, really, considering the hundreds of days she had spent racing through twenty-hour shifts as an intern. Why should half a day's work after a couple of days off seem so tough?

Knowing the answer lay in the memory of how she had spent the previous sixty hours—and with whom—she downed the soda, plopped into one of the aluminum chairs and put her elbows on the card table. Half her strength had gone into trying to forget.

The other half had been spent dealing with older Navajo patients who hadn't wanted her help. Two had come in to the Raven Wash Clinic for help but refused to have a *bilagáana* woman tend them.

Not even the seventy-year-old man who had been sliced by barbed wire and needed a total of forty-two sutures to close up the many deep cuts along his face, arms and hands had wanted to be treated by a white woman doctor.

A Navajo nurse and Tory's own inept attempt at a few Navajo words had finally calmed him down enough for her to get the job done. But it had taken a lot out of her.

The whole thing might've been much easier if her stomach hadn't been rolling over a nagging worry that the future looked muddy as hell. Would Ben beat his eye disease?

A couple of things about him were plain, though. Like the fact that the two of them would never be a couple for the long haul. And even for the short haul he'd managed to make the idea sound impossible. Would he continue to let her be his friend and help him out?

She was still driving his SUV, and now she also had the cell phone he'd sent to the clinic. So she guessed that must mean she wasn't out of his life forever—yet.

Tory had gone straight to Dr. Hardeen this morning to ask for permission to work with Ben two or three days a week. Her boss said he was pleased to give her the time, and suggested a full-time leave for a month or two away from the Raven Wash Clinic.

In fact, he had seemed a little too happy about losing his white woman doctor. It made her wonder if he might be relieved to get a break from dealing with patients who balked at her treatment. That couldn't be easy for him to deal with every day.

The only thing she had ever wanted out of life was to be a healer. What would she do if she had to spend the next three years on the sidelines, advising other doctors and nurses but not treating patients?

She vowed to keep practicing more Navajo words and hoped that working with Ben would help teach her more about their ways. At least enough to get by with patients.

As for now…she eyed the computer terminal blinking away in a dark corner of the break room. It was mainly used for research and online contact with distant specialists, and Tory figured it wouldn't hurt anything for her to check her e-mail and see if either of the people she'd contacted yesterday from the high school had gotten back to her yet.

Maybe one of them would be able to offer Ben more than just someone to drive him around and a tentative friendship. Maybe one of them would actually come up with a real solution.

Ben rode shotgun in Lucas Tso's pickup as they drove the firebreak along the top of Crystal Mesa on their way to talk to a few relatives of the boy who had died at the wrestling match.

Foolishly, he'd been staring out at the violet-and-peach streaks of clouds silhouetted across the robin's-egg blue sky. Worse yet, he'd even been admiring and soaking up the deep evergreen colors of ponderosa pines and the wispy light tan of aspens.

Foolish of him to be enjoying it so much. Because the very minute he thought of how wonderful it was to be able to see such a sight, his eyesight failed him again.

Thrown once more into the black hole of blindness, Ben was left with only the memories. And the very first memory to surface from the recesses of his mind was of cobalt sparks, flaming from soft gray-blue eyes.

He flashed right back to the dim light of early morning. To the point when he'd regained his sight and had focused on watching Tory's reactions as he made love to her.

The rose flush of her cheeks as her passion hit had sent him to a higher place. The pale golden beauty of the tender skin on her rib cage. The hidden treasures of reddish-brown freckles that he'd discovered secreted on her mid-back—all were wondrous sights he would never forget.

The flashbacks grew more intimate and took him back to whispered sighs and tender caresses. To heated gasps when the electricity singed them both. To her salty, honey and tangy tastes.

And finally, to shadowed smiles, ear-blasting shrieks and soothing embraces as their breaths mingled in the aftershocks.

Hell. He couldn't see a damned thing at this point. It would be crazy for him to continue hiding it from the Brotherhood. They needed to know now that he was not as capable of helping out as he had been before.

"I have an eye disease that is growing worse," he told Lucas. "Soon I may not be able to see at all."

"I know." Lucas Tso, a tall, lean Navajo with an artistic temperament and a fierce loyalty to the Brotherhood, drove on without turning. "I have sensed your new impairment on occasion. But it changes little when it comes to our war with the Skinwalkers. In fact, it may make you more alert to the dangers around you."

"I believe it's more of a weakness than you think," Ben told him. "I can't see a thing right now. How will I be able to help question the Yellow House Clan relatives of that teenager who died?"

"You will listen. Listen for truth. Listen for small discrepancies and for uncomfortable silences.

"The *heart* of the Brotherhood dwells in empathy," Lucas continued. "You must learn to *judge* without seeing who could be the true enemy. The *evil ones* lurk in seeming innocence around you. Use your other senses to find them."

Yes, well, he was becoming better and better at using some of those other senses. In fact, it took every power he could muster to keep from thinking about how those other senses had been engaged just last night. But there was no question at all of Tory being the enemy. Not a possibility.

Ben sat back in the seat and let the hot wind from the open pickup window blow against his face. He closed his eyes and concentrated on the smell of creosote and thick red earth.

He would do what he could. Be what he could be. That was the Navajo Way.

And he would absolutely stop being so absorbed by the colors in the strands of cornsilk hair or in a pair of intelligent, flashing eyes.

Tory headed for the break room at the end of her shift. She hoped to find a message on her e-mail from the other former professor she'd contacted about help for Ben.

Her pharmacology professor had already answered and

said he knew of no studies being done for a cure of azoor disease. He had added something else interesting, though. It seemed he had heard rumors from a buddy who worked for an international drug company. The rumor concerned a secret cure for some deadly disease that had supposedly been discovered by a research lab on the Navajo reservation.

The drug-world blogs and grapevines were all abuzz. Doubts and misgivings aside, it seemed the drug company was about to pay big bucks for more research. Interesting, but of no help for Ben.

She stuck her head through the break-room door, hoping for a chance at the computer to see if her Pathology of Rare Eye Diseases professor had gotten back to her yet. But instead of an empty room she found nurse Russel, sitting in front of the computer with his back to her.

"Excuse me, Russel, but I'm leaving for the day. You should be happy, too, because I'm going home long before dark."

He jerked as if he'd been shot, quickly flipped off the computer screen as though he wanted to hide what he'd been doing and swiveled his chair around so he could glare at her. "Fine, Dr. Sommer. Good evening."

It made her more than a little curious, wondering what he might've been looking at online. "What were you just doing?" she asked and stepped closer to him. "You weren't contacting a specialist concerning a patient, were you? I haven't seen any charts for anyone whose condition might need a consultation. Did I miss something?"

He straightened his back and narrowed his eyes. "Not at all. I was just doing a bit of personal research. Nothing to concern yourself over." Lifting his head, he stared down his beak of a nose and pinned her in his black gaze.

Holy crap. April had been right. Russel did look like a bird of prey getting ready to pounce on a meal.

Only the kind of fowl he resembled was more along the lines of a ferocious black raven. The glare in those beady dark eyes of his reminded her instantly of the sight of an odd raven as it had perched on the roof of Ben's house.

It sent a shiver down her spine. "I…uh…I won't be coming in much for the next few weeks," she managed to stutter as she took a step backward.

"No? I assume Dr. Hardeen has approved your request for time off."

"It's not any of your business, but no, I'm not taking time off. I'll be helping Dr. Wauneka out with a few things at his clinic."

"I see." Russel swirled his chair toward the computer screen again. "If you were thinking of asking if we'll be okay without you, the answer is yes. We'll be fine here."

He dismissed her by keeping his back turned. "Just remember my advice, Doctor, and stay off the roads at night."

Son of a…

Damn, was she ever glad she wouldn't be dealing with arrogant, creepy Russel for the next few weeks. She stormed down the corridor as fast as she could go.

But the minute she cleared the outside door and headed into the warmth of the late-afternoon sun, she thought about facing a steel-edged Navajo doctor whose warm brown eyes refused to focus. And decided that might be every bit as difficult to do. But in a different way.

She'd barely climbed into the driver's seat of Ben's SUV and shut the door behind her when her purse started ringing. Or rather, her brand-new cell phone must've been ringing.

Digging the jangling thing out of her purse, she found the talk button and pushed. "Hello?"

"*Ya'at'eeh,* Doctor. This is the Plant Tender calling. There is still plenty of light. Would you have the time now for a lesson?"

Shirley Nez. The woman's generous warm smile came through, even on the phone.

"I have time. But I don't know yet if Ben will need me to give him a ride home, or if I'll have to give him a place to stay for the night. Maybe I should call—"

"The doctor will not be going home tonight—the road to his house is still unpassable. And he has made arrangements to stay with cousins for the evening. You are free to learn."

Trying to stifle a disappointed groan, Tory took the directions for getting to Shirley's house and hung up.

Freedom was the one thing she'd had plenty of since the very first day she left home for college. Free to come and go. Free to work from dawn to dawn and as hard as any man. Free to break any personal commitments that didn't suit her lifestyle.

And free to know icy isolation and to be all alone.

She was there, in his dreams, the minute he finally fell off to sleep. It wasn't so much the sight of her as it was her essence that captured Ben's midnight hours.

It had a been a frustrating day of getting no answers. But the night was proving to be just as frustrating.

With hot, shaking-the-bed and roll-around dreams, he'd awoken several times hard and sweaty—and furious with himself. He could see her so clearly, with that blond hair streaming down and tickling his stomach as she leaned over him. See her with perfect vision, digging her nails into his arms as he had used them to pin hers over her head so he could dip into her tastes once more.

He wasn't sure he'd really seen any of it. Or if all the images had been burned into his mind by the intensity of their union.

Had he really seen her licking her lips in anticipation of kissing his erection? Had he really beheld the gleam in her eyes as she fit him inside and let her internal muscles suck him ever deeper?

Sitting straight up in his cousin Lucas's spare bed, he was embarrassed by his current physical condition. Good thing he was alone. He'd been so close to losing the ultimate control, right here, all alone.

Ben flipped on his stomach and pounded the pillow into flattened submission. No fair. The one woman who he could've found a real spiritual and physical connection to had to be an Anglo.

Figured. A doctor without sight. A crystal gazer without vision. A warrior without the ability to see the enemy.

Why the hell shouldn't he also be the man who'd found a perfect lover but would forever be unable to have her?

Sighing, he knew there would be no more sleeping for him tonight.

Exhausted from listening to Shirley's lessons and trying to memorize both plant lore and the Navajo words, Tory got ready for bed. But after she'd brushed her teeth, shut off the lights and headed down the hall, she knew it would be impossible to sleep in *that* bed tonight.

Too many hot memories and warm feelings for her to go into her own bedroom.

Making a U-turn before stepping through the door, she found her way in the dark to the suede couch in her great room. Afraid to close her eyes for fear she would re-member everything—much too clearly—she curled up and pulled an afghan over her legs.

Sighing, she stared out into the black stillness of her house. And knew there would be no sleeping for her tonight.

Chapter 11

A week later Tory glanced up into Ben's eyes and knew his vision had returned—for the moment.

But the lines around those beautiful chocolate eyes of his had grown deeper in the last few days, and the grooves across his forehead were more furrowed and narrowed to a point between his eyebrows. He looked as tired as she felt.

It made her wonder if he'd been sleeping well. She knew she hadn't been. She'd been commuting the hour and a half both ways up here to his mountain clinic every day, and then spending every extra minute of the late afternoons with Shirley Nez. Exhausted, Tory ought to be tired enough to collapse into bed at night and be asleep before her head hit the pillow.

She wasn't. Tossing and turning and worrying about Ben made up most of her dark-time hours. What was *he* doing or not doing that was causing his current exhausted look?

She'd always been able to look as if she was handling the loss of a little sleep. Ben, on the other hand, appeared stressed and tense—and worried.

What had done that to him? His off-and-on blindness that seemed less and less likely for a reprieve?

Or was there something more? Certainly he couldn't be feeling the same irritating exasperation at the unwanted memories of one wild night as she was. It was a single night, for heaven's sake. Lots of people had one-night stands and kept on working together. She'd seen it done dozens of times back at the hospital in Chicago.

Of course, she'd also seen an occasional explosion of feelings from such pairings that ruined careers and sent one or more of the participants off to distant places in order to get away from the embarrassment. But that wouldn't apply to her and Ben. She simply refused to let one night and lots of confusing feelings stop her from helping him and trying to be his friend.

She needed him—to teach her about living and working with the Dine—almost as much as he needed her to guide him through his darkness. So some small tension between them could not stop them from working together.

Or from searching for answers to his cure. That was what she did, after all. She tended people and found ways of making them better.

Nothing had materialized on the cure front yet. But the biggest setback to her plans had been discovering that she quaked every time he had to take her hand. And that happened a lot in order for her to guide him. She also continued to be damned unhappy about feeling anxious and itchy whenever they were in close quarters.

Like they were right now, standing hip to hip and bandaging a young boy who had been mauled by a dog. But the ten-year-old's sutures were already in place. The tetanus shot and a first rabies vaccination had been administered, and the boy's trauma was nearing an end.

"I've got this," he told her. "Can you go calm down his aunt? I'll be able to get to her in a minute or two."

Tory nodded, and was pleased to know he saw her do it. She was also pleased to be able to converse with the middle-aged woman on the bench outside by way of a few Navajo words. She'd learned quite a lot in the last week. Just a few well-chosen phrases, said correctly, went a long way toward making Ben's patients feel more comfortable with her.

When Tory stepped out past the blanketed door, she found the woman collapsed on the ground. Tory quickly checked her pulse and respiration. The woman's heart was pounding but her breathing seemed normal.

Tory turned back to the door and called for Ben's help. Between them, they got the woman into the medicine hogan and laid her on an examining table as she began to come back to consciousness.

It only took a few minutes of examination for Tory to diagnose the woman as probably having hyperventilated, worrying about her nephew. Her blood pressure was slightly elevated, her pupils still dilated. But she was calming now and should be okay in a few minutes.

Making a decision based on a week's worth of watching Ben work with patients, Tory decided to remain silent and let him do the talking. It was entirely possible the woman had low blood sugar and Ben already knew she should be watched more closely.

"What happened to you?" he asked the woman who was now sitting up.

"It's my heart. The boy and I...we have the ghost sickness."

"Your nephew was attacked by a vicious dog. It was a dog, wasn't it?"

The woman nodded her head. "Yes, while we were out with my brother's sheep this morning. But it was a dog witch. It disappeared right away."

Tory saw the woman go pale, reaching for her heart, so she stepped closer to her side. Was there some real underlying illness here? The woman's heart sounded strong enough. But Tory put her arm around her shoulder, giving her support.

"Please get Mrs. Yellowhorse a drink of water," Ben asked Tory.

She backed away from the patient and did as he requested.

"I am going to check you over," he told the woman. "The crystal will tell us if this is ghost sickness or not. What do you believe the two of you have done to deserve to be witched?"

Mrs. Yellowhorse's eyes grew wide. "We...it was an accident. A few days ago. We were searching for one of the lost lambs in an arroyo near Tocito Wash. It is one my brother does not usually use for sheep. My nephew and I hadn't intended to disturb the—Wolf."

Tory saw Ben's sudden stillness. Heard his slight intake of breath. And couldn't imagine what had been said that seemed so strange to him. Wild animals like a wolf must be a rather common sight out in these remote wilderness areas. Was he concerned the woman was developing an acute form of mental illness or hysteria?

Ben reached for one of his crystals, the ones she'd seen him use once or twice before to soothe an elderly patient.

"You saw the Navajo Wolf?" he asked gently. "Did he threaten you? Touch you?"

The woman shook her head. "No, but he came near enough to see. We heard him talk. Saw that he had—destroyed the lamb." She shivered at the memory. "We left quickly, but the damage was already done."

Tory stood quietly while Ben looked through the large clear crystal and ran it over the woman's chest area. The patient lay very still and waited for him to make a diagnosis.

Surprised to see him surreptitiously watching the woman's respiration and reflexes as he moved the crystal around, Tory remained quiet as Ben drew the glass back and forth from her heart to head. With the crystal hovering about two inches above the patient's clothing, Ben kept speaking softly in Navajo words Tory didn't understand.

The entire process took about fifteen minutes.

Finally Ben lifted his chin and smiled at Mrs. Yellowhorse. "You do not have ghost sickness, but you are troubled and the dark wind is affecting your heart. I will speak to a *hataalii* on your behalf. You and the boy need a full Blessing Way ceremony."

The woman managed a sharp nod and squeezed her eyes closed.

"But while you are here," Ben continued gently, "I'll perform a Song of Blessing and will give you both Life Way medicines. They'll help bring you peace until the longer ceremony can be arranged."

Those words appeared to have an immediate calming effect on the woman. She uncrunched her face and her skin began to lose its gray pallor as the cheeks took on a touch of real color. Ben asked Tory to wait outside while he performed his ceremony.

Tory sat on the benches by the door, and listened as Ben chanted in a low voice. The ceremony lasted slightly under an hour. Meanwhile, she raised her face to the warmth of the sun and watched while a couple of big birds circled gracefully high in the sky overhead.

Sitting there, she had plenty of time to think about dog witches and Navajo wolves. To think about the power of the mind both to cause illness and to cure it.

But there was also way too much time for her to worry about a hard-steeled but gentle man who knew how to make people well—but who couldn't cure his own looming illness.

And it made her almost weep in frustration.

"I had trouble getting around the house alone again last night," Ben said in a quiet tone as Tory drove them toward Big Sky canyon. "The blindness is lasting for longer and longer time periods. Will you reconsider staying overnight?"

He held his breath and waited for her answer. It had been the truth about the hours of growing darkness. But of course, he knew he could always get a cousin to come stay with him. Ben didn't want a cousin, though. He wanted Tory.

Checking her profile with a quick glance, he fought the heat that seeing her always caused. Still, with his first glimpse of her sunny yellow hair, the need licked at his libido and made furious desire an unwanted distraction.

As usual.

But, damn. Today she'd worn her blond hair swept up in some kind of clip, leaving the tender skin on the back of her long neck exposed—and too tantalizing. While the tip of her nose, pinked from all her hours in the sun with Shirley, just begged to be kissed.

How many more times would he be capable of looking over this way and seeing her sitting there?

Not many, he feared. His attention wavered momentarily as he quit breathing and drank in the sight of her. She just had to stop leaving him for so many long, lonely hours every day. He needed her to stay by his side.

What's more, he was afraid for her safety when she wasn't nearby. His sense of a danger coming ever closer to both of them had grown acute. He'd even spoken to a couple of the other Brotherhood members about his unusual feeling of unease. Some of them had suggested that both he and Tory should never be allowed to be alone without the other or without a Brotherhood member.

Fine by him.

"I…" she began hesitantly. "All right. I'll bring some clothes and overnight necessities along tomorrow when I come up. I can stay here just as well as I can down in that house by Bluebird Ridge. At least until you can get someone else on a more permanent basis.

"I've been increasingly concerned about you being alone at night." She'd added that last comment with what sounded to Ben like a soft sigh of resignation.

He laid a gentle hand on her arm and stared at her long lashes while they blinked furiously. "Will it be such a chore to be with me for more hours every day?"

She sucked in a tiny breath and jerked her arm away as if his touch had burned her. "No…I wouldn't say that. It's going to be okay."

What would she say if she knew the truth? The truth he had to admit to himself during the darkest parts of his time alone.

She was his destiny. Somehow he knew that with a crazy certainty—a certainty born out of his romantic

Navajo traditions. The idea had been in the back of his head since the first minute he'd seen her.

The original lust he'd felt—still felt when he didn't dwell on it too much—had somehow expanded and deepened. It had taken on shades, colors, even textures all its own.

But to his mind, a long-term relationship was simply not going to happen between them. No possible way.

So, he was bound to lose this woman—his other half— one day. In fact, he could picture himself actually sending her away on some black day in the near future. Between trying to follow his mother's teachings and the ever-threatening cloud of the Skinwalker war, she didn't belong with him in Dinetah for good.

And just where would that leave him? All alone in the darkness—forever.

Perhaps they were supposed to come together in an afterlife. To be joined for all eternity as they could not be while here in the earthly lands between the four sacred mountains.

Ben took a huge cleansing breath and tried to shake away the too-poetic thoughts from his brain. Desperate to find some balance to keep him straight in the coming darkness, he decided he would much rather lose the romanticism, thank you very much. It would be better for him to simply go back to his original gut-twisting combo of lust and need, for however much time they had left.

She turned the wheel to miss a pothole and cleared her throat. "Will we be away from your office through the whole afternoon today?"

"Yes," he managed to answer as he dragged his attention toward the front window of the SUV. "Maybe until late in the evening, if you don't mind."

Laughing, she turned to him. His head swung around just in time to catch a certain depth underneath the twinkle in her eyes that he hadn't seen before.

"So you're going to let me drive down to the house on Bluebird Ridge alone *in the dark* after I drop you off later tonight?" she quipped.

"I was hoping you'd start staying over with me tonight and go down to your house for the things you need tomorrow."

"Right. I figured as much." She moved her attention back to the road ahead. "But I thought we were just driving over to visit a patient of yours this afternoon. That teen whose grandmother came in to see you yesterday. A house call can't possibly take more than a hour or two. Can it?"

"I doubt it. But that isn't all I'd hoped to do today."

She tilted her head in that endearing way she had and grinned. "Okay. What else have you got planned?"

Hell. How was he ever going to manage when the time came and he would never be able to see her do that again?

"I...we...have been invited to a Night Way Ceremony that will be taking place later this afternoon," he told her haltingly. "It'll no doubt run on late into the night. And I wanted you to be able to participate in a ceremony like this one. Get a feel for some of the old public Sings. They aren't held on the Reservation much anymore."

In truth, he'd wanted to see one himself again, too. Maybe for the last time. Before long he would only be able to listen to the chants and have mere memories of the sights.

"What's a Night Way Ceremony all about?"

"It's a coming-of-age celebration. Kids, age eleven or so, go through this as they are entering puberty. I have both a female and a male cousin who will be celebrating tonight."

"Am I dressed all right for it? I mean, I didn't expect to be going to a party."

He shot a glance down her body, taking in the plaid work shirt rolled up to her elbows and the soft light-blue jeans hugging curves he remembered much too fondly. "You're fine. I'll ask one of my aunts if you can borrow a traditional skirt if it makes you more comfortable, though."

"Thanks. I'm really looking forward to seeing my first ceremony and meeting more of your family. It was nice of you to think of me." She eased on the brake and hiccupped a laugh. "Or am I just the driver who has to be there to take you home? They do know I'm coming along, don't they?"

"Oh, they know." And every single female in his extended family would be taking stock of the white woman doctor. While every single male would be wanting to get closer to her.

He sighed and leaned back in the seat. But none of them would be going home with her—and he would. Thanks in no small measure to his old friend and terrible nemesis, his destiny.

Tory eased farther back into the shadows of the curtains in the front room of the hot aluminum trailer house. She remained quiet while she listened to Ben ask his young patient a few questions. The two males were speaking softly in English, as the teenager had looked decidedly uncomfortable speaking Navajo around the white woman doctor.

The sight of Ben, dressed in what she'd come to think of as his *hataalii* outfit, gave her a sense of well-being. The deep maroon long-sleeved shirt tucked inside clean jeans made him seem intelligent and wise. The pale blue scarf around his forehead and the long hair tied back in the semblance of a bun made him look traditional and very much Native American.

The concho belt he wore and the twin sets of turquoise-and-silver bracelets on each arm made him appear strong and—secure. That just had to be a better word to use than *sexy,* which was where her brain had wandered.

The young man they had come to see looked to be about sixteen. He, too, seemed strong and intelligent. A tall, strapping kid with broad shoulders and huge feet the rest of him hadn't grown into yet, the boy appeared as healthy as a horse. It made Tory wonder why they were here.

"Your grandmother tells me you're trying to make a choice in the direction of your life. Your life's Way," Ben said to the teenager. "So you want to talk about it?"

The kid grimaced and shook his head. "She shouldn't have called you. I've made the choice."

Ben squatted beside the boy's chair. "There is always the possibility of new choices. Or changed thoughts on different ways to go."

"In a couple of days it will be too late to change my mind," the teenager said in a haughty way. "In fact, my mind is already made up. No real need to go into it anymore. Sorry to make you come out of your way."

"You intend to begin taking steroids to bulk up then," Ben said as he shook his head. "Who's going to get them for you?"

"It's more than just that," the kid said with a wave of his hand. "I'm joining a gang that will take care of me for the rest of my life. I won't ever have to worry about going to college or even about getting a job. My posse will watch my back from now on. I won't be needing a damned *hataalii* or any frigging Navajo mumbo-jumbo, either."

Tory's head came up. Steroids and teen gangs? Remembering her discussion with the young girl at the high school, she decided to pay closer attention to what was being said. When she'd asked Ben about the athletes and drug use later on that day, he'd told her that the Brotherhood knew all about it and would be taking care of the problem. He'd said for her not to worry.

But now this didn't much sound like the problem was going away.

Ben turned his head toward her and she saw a shadow ripple across his features. A stricken look burned in his eyes. Talking about the teenage secret society was obviously very hard for him.

"Maybe you don't yet have all the facts," he told the boy gently. "Are you aware that it's adults who are directing that group? It *isn't* the kids in charge."

The boy's chin jerked up, and Tory was sure she saw the first signs of a break in his determination. "Sure," the kid muttered hesitantly. "Of course I knew that's what those old guys think. But the posse is using old guys like Coach Singleton and that other medicine hotshot dude to get the drugs and money. No big problemo. We've got it covered."

"What other medicine hotshot dude?" Ben asked a little too sharply.

The kid shrugged and averted his eyes. "Didn't catch his name, but it doesn't matter. They just get the drug stuff and show us how to use it. There's this whole big ceremony involved when you join up." The kid laughed. "Sort of beating the likes of you at your own mumbling game, *hataalii.*"

"Have you been to any of these ceremonies yet?" Ben asked in a lower tone. "Talked to anyone who's been?"

The kid's eyes suddenly went dark with obvious fear. "Uh, no. The guys who've gone don't need to talk to us recruits anymore. They're already in the big time."

Lowering his voice to a near whisper, the boy continued. "I've heard there's hazing you have to live through," he managed with a rasp. "But the drugs are supposed to give you the strength to get past it. Once you're on the other side, you don't need your regular clan family or your old buddies ever again."

"What kind of hazing? Have you heard rumors?"

Now the kid's demeanor suddenly seemed downright scared. His shoulders slumped and he hung his head.

Ben stood and put a firm hand on his shoulder. "You don't have to say it, son. I know."

"You don't know anything." It was a last comeback for a kid who must be able to feel he wasn't going to get what he wanted. The adults would win yet another battle.

"It's no disgrace for you to be afraid," Ben murmured to him. "But I want you to promise me you won't go to one of these ceremonies until I can get another *hataalii* up here to bring you a special talisman to protect you. Is it a deal?"

"Why should I?" The terror was written all over the petrified teen.

"Because you don't want to have to face that horror without a little special protection on your side, do you?"

The kid kept his head down, but shook it slightly.

"Fine," Ben said soberly. "In the meantime, I wouldn't leave the house at night if I were you. You won't have a chance if you come across one of them before you are protected. You know there's no hiding from Skinwalkers."

Chapter 12

Ben sat in the passenger seat of his SUV. Lost in thought, he stared absently out the window at the dazzling sunshine bouncing off the familiar sienna cliffs in the distance.

The minute he and Tory had left the teen's trailer, he'd excused himself to call the Brotherhood. He reached Hunter Long, who told him the problem of the Skinwalker cult was already known and arrangements were being made.

He'd also said that Lucas and a few of the others would come to rescue the teenager later today. Hunter mentioned then that several men of the Brotherhood were closing in on Coach Singleton, but the man had taken off.

The "society" would be broken up soon and most of the kids rounded up within twenty-four hours. The teenage boys would all be put through special detox with sacred Navajo plants, and any lingering brainwashing would be dealt with on a case-by-case basis.

But Ben's uneasy spirit refused to be stilled. The Skin-walkers had chosen to pick on children. On boys who hadn't yet had their hopes and dreams dashed against the reality of life on the rez. Damn them.

All of his life Ben had been conditioned to the Navajo Way of not seeking revenge. People were never to be hated for what they did. Those who violated basic rules of civilized behavior simply had a "dark wind" in them that needed to be controlled and removed.

Ben fisted his hands and jammed them hard against his thighs. He was having a difficult time not hating those Skinwalker bastards. Dark wind, hell. Was this all simply about greed? Ruined lives and terrorized children—because of money?

"Can I ask something?" Tory's voice broke into his thoughts.

"Ask. I may not be able to give you the answer you want, however."

"Do you really think a talisman of some sort will protect that boy from a hazing?" She didn't even take a breath before the rest of her questions spilled out into the warm air between them. "And I thought you told me that the Brotherhood was looking into that society at Raven Wash High. This is the same one, right? Who is Coach Singleton? And do you have any ideas about the person in 'medicine' who is getting the drugs for those kids?"

Ben sat quietly and waited as she wound down. He'd been right. The woman of his destiny was too damned bright.

He searched his brain for half answers that might work to stop her questions for the time being. She wasn't ready for the whole truth. Maybe she never would be.

"Don't worry about that teen," he said at last. "None of the boys will be going to any more hazing ceremonies.

This so-called society is nothing more than a cult. Now that we know about it, the cult will be dismantled and the boys will be deprogrammed and sent to detox. Within a few days, there won't be a problem.

"The harder question is how to give these kids more of a chance at a better future," Ben added. "Poverty and little opportunity for higher education will continue to put our kids at risk for drug and gang problems."

Tory kept her eyes focused on the road and maintained a steady speed up the side of Badwash cliff. "I understand. It's a shame—the kids I've met seem so bright. But what about the adults? What will happen to this Coach Singleton? Who is he anyway?"

"He's the head coach at Raven Wash High, and—"

She interrupted him with a gasp. "Not April Henry's fiancé? Oh, poor April. He's bound to go to jail. I'm sure she has no idea what he's been doing."

It didn't take Tory another thirty seconds to think of her next question. "Do you or the Brotherhood have any clues about the 'medicine dude' that kid was talking about? Is it someone we might know?"

"It's being looked into."

That answer slowed her down. But Ben could see it wasn't the answer she sought. And he knew more questions were forming inside her head as she drove along the top of the hill into the brilliant sun.

Her last question had been a good one, though. In his opinion, the best one in the bunch of her queries. Was it a medicine *man?* Or someone *in* medicine. Like a doctor or a nurse or maybe a pharmacist?

Perhaps the Brotherhood would be able to find out as they questioned the teenagers they were rounding up. Ben decided to give it a lot more thought himself.

"And for heaven's sake, tell me what the heck a Skinwalker is," Tory asked, jolting him from his thoughts. "I've never even heard the term, but it sure seemed to scare that poor kid. He was out of his wits with fright by the time you were done with him."

Ben had been biding his time waiting for that question. Trouble was, he still didn't have an adequate answer.

"I told you once there were some legends and concepts in Dinetah that would be difficult for you to grasp," he began as steadily as possible. "The Skinwalker legend is a part of our culture, and has been for a thousand years or more. But it's a very long story, and I'd rather rest a while now before I participate in the Night Way chant tonight.

"I'll tell you the whole legend another day," he continued, hoping the wary tone of his voice would sound just plain weary to Tory. "Not right now, though. Do you mind?"

"Oh, I didn't realize you would be participating in the ceremony tonight. Yes, please rest. We can talk about it another day."

Ben closed his eyes and leaned back against the headrest, glad he'd dodged the bullet for now. But he knew she wouldn't give it up forever. Tory had proven to be intensely tenacious when something bothered her.

He shook his head and tried to hide the inappropriate smile he couldn't stop. She was just too damn bright.

Sitting on an old tree stump in the plum-colored dusk, Tory watched Ben's family and friends from a distance and reflected on her interesting afternoon. There hadn't been a moment since they'd arrived here on the clan's ceremonial mesa for her to think about steroids or teenage cults. And she still couldn't bring herself to dwell on such depressing thoughts.

Not when the gaudy red sunset was still peering teasingly over a distant mountain peak. She had never witnessed such a profusion of colors. The whole of the afternoon had dazzled her with a whirl of sights and sounds and smells.

She'd met Navajos of every age, with skin and eyes in a thousand different color combinations. Nutmeg, cinnamon, mocha, bronze, even a color Tory would have to name cognac. Women with raven hair and ebony eyes and dressed in multicolored long skirts so brilliant and exciting they competed with the scenery for attention had cooked and chatted and laughed all afternoon long.

Her ears had been assaulted by heavy male chants. Then low-pitched songs from both sexes had been sung to the *Yei* gods, whose vibrant-colored masks had been worn in the earlier ceremony. The spicy smells she'd identified as smoke and sage and pine. Going on sensory overload, she was glad to have found a spot to catch her breath.

Wanting to locate Ben, she easily spotted him surrounded by family and at the center of their attention. A lump formed in her throat as she watched him laughing and interacting with both elders and young children.

She found herself bombarded with emotion and need as she continued to stare at him. Feelings chased through her that were so foreign they might as well be from Mars.

Trying to sort them out, the first one she identified, of course, was sexual need. That gleam of desire whenever he was around tickled her like an old friend. Ben's image enchanted her mind with memories both soft and sharp, electrifying and numbing.

But she was adult enough to keep those needs from coming between them or from interrupting their tenuous friendship. It was more the hidden emotions, underlying the lust, that were harder to define. Finally, she dropped the ancient walls around her heart and just admitted she was *jealous* of him. Crazy, right?

But there it was. Watching him surrounded by people he loved and who loved and respected him in return. Knowing he felt his roots and traditions every minute he was standing on Dine land. It made her, well…feel left out.

That *was* crazy. She'd been raised in a huge Irish-American family and couldn't possibly ache to belong to yet another big group. But she did.

Her own family had never understood her. When she'd decided to become a doctor, her brothers had all assumed it was because of the money she could make. She'd tried to explain, but none of them ever understood. Just as her ex had never really gotten into her true motivations, either.

None of them spoke the same language as she did. They talked dollars. She talked about making a difference.

Navajo had turned out to be a much easier language for her to learn.

She kept watching as two youngsters with long ebony hair came over to Ben and threw their arms around his waist. They grinned up into his eyes and Tory detected another subtle shift in her feelings.

This time, when her heart finally put a name on the emotion, she forced herself to admit it was love. Though she was sure she'd never experienced such a thing before, the feeling she'd just dug up from the depths of her gut had to be what other people called *love*.

What else would cause this desperate need to please

him—beyond any consideration for her own pleasure? To protect him—even at the cost of her own well-being?

As if he could hear her thoughts, Ben lifted his head and sought her out. When their gazes met and locked, the tension sparked between them as if it was a live electric wire. The intense heat, the meeting of minds and hearts in agreement—she felt all that and much more in every tendon and muscle of her body.

He turned and started in her direction. With each step he took, her temperature increased by degrees.

"Are you okay?" he asked as he got closer.

Her first impulse was to simply nod her head because her throat was tight with emotion.

But she'd trained herself to speak aloud in case he couldn't see her movements. "Yes. And you? How's your vision?"

"So far, so good. I'm sorry for leaving you on your own. I couldn't seem to break away from ceremonial duties. Are you unhappy you came?"

"Not a bit. I enjoyed watching the ceremony, and the food has been terrific. All your family has been most kind. Can you sit with me for a while now and explain some of the things I've seen?"

"Well…*I* could. But *your* presence has been requested by my great-uncle, Hastiin Lakai Begay of the Salt Clan for the Big Medicine People. He's the family patriarch and we have some trouble telling him no. Do you mind?"

"My presence? Without you there?" She had a moment of pure panic. "You know my Navajo is not very good. What could he want from me?"

Ben laughed, and the sound was so sweet that her fears fled in a rush of warm goodwill.

"Don't worry about the language," he told her with a

wave of dismissal. "Uncle Lakai speaks perfect English—when he wants to. And he's nearly blind these days, so he's not threatening in the least."

"Blind? Not…"

Once again Ben laughed. "No. His blindness is quite normal for a man of his age. Macular degeneration. Nothing exotic. But he does tend to use it sometimes to explain away his more…uh…eccentric behaviors.

"And as for what he wants from you," Ben continued with a smile, "no doubt he wants you to be a fresh audience. Uncle Lakai is the family storyteller. All of us have heard his tales so many times that we have trouble sitting through them anymore."

Ben crooked his elbow and offered it to her when she stood to follow him. "You probably aren't going to like knowing this," he told her in a conspiratorial tone. "But the traditional Navajo way of storytelling means that no *one* teller ever finishes the tale. It's an ancient social custom, meant to give everyone a chance to be the star for a time. It can be rather frustrating unless there's a circle of storytellers standing by ready to finish up."

"You're kidding," she sputtered with a laugh of her own. "So nobody gets to tell their own punch line?"

Ben shook his head, but his eyes were sparkling with mischief. "Not with the oldest generation, no. Don't worry, though. One of the younger, more modern generations will be happy to fill you in if it's a legend we know."

"And if it's not?"

She looked up at his profile just in time to see a wry grin. "If it's not, then I guess we'll just have to teach you how to have a Navajo imagination so you can make up your own ending."

Terrific. First the language, then the plant remedies

and the legends, and now she had to get a Navajo imagination, too? Whoo, boy. She had most definitely dropped
out of the sky and *wasn't in Kansas anymore, scarecrow.*

Ben had been so proud of Tory that he nearly pledged
his undying allegiance right there on the spot in front
of the entire clan. When he'd introduced her to his formidable
uncle Lakai, she'd greeted the elder with a few well-pro-
nounced Navajo phrases and made the man an admirer for
life.

As with the rest of his clan, ninety-year-old Hastiin
Lakai Begay was enthralled to meet the blond doctor who
was trying so hard not to stand out from the crowd. Tory
might not know it, but that was also a big part of the traditional Navajo Way. Fitting in. Belonging.

Ben loved her for somehow empirically knowing that
tradition and for being the kind of person who would care
about such things. He…hell, he just loved her for who she
was.

But he caught himself wishing for an answer to the
problem of some day having to set aside his love. Ben was
more and more convinced that losing her in the end would
be completely devastating. Forcing himself to shove the
growing concern about it out of his mind, he had to find a
way to move ahead with his life and live more in the
moment.

Settling her and Uncle Lakai down on a couple of camp
chairs behind one of the newly lit bonfires, Ben asked one
of the women to bring them the traditional cups of coffee
that were a big part of the storytellers' tradition. Then he
left them to get acquainted. He found it hard to walk away
from her side for any reason.

But he needed a few minutes to talk to some of his

cousins in the Brotherhood who were attending tonight's clan ceremony. Hunter, Kody and Michael Ayze were waiting for him to start the strategic planning session concerning their next moves in the Skinwalker war. The men also needed to discuss the potential suspects who might be qualified as the "medicine dude" that the teenager had mentioned.

It was important to track down any leads about the ones who looked like Navajos most of the time but who could turn into Skinwalker witches at will. More than important, actually. It was a matter of life and death. The life and death of the entire Navajo Nation.

"You are the one who is working with the Plant Tender?" Uncle Lakai asked as he sipped his coffee.

The question surprised Tory into a few seconds of stunned silence. She'd been expecting questions about her relationship to Ben, or about her plans for the future on the reservation, or even about current research being done on macular degeneration. But the question about Shirley took her back.

"I've been learning the plants and remedies from Shirley Nez, yes. I find it an interesting and pleasant occupation."

Uncle Lakai had both hands wrapped around his steaming mug of coffee. But as he lowered the mug, he turned his face in her direction. Blank, black eyes stared out over the top of her head.

"Lessons are much more than simply pleasant and interesting for the future Plant Tender," he said abruptly.

Before she could ask what he meant, he began again, "I have sight."

"Excuse me?" Was he talking about getting his own vision back?

"I have 'seen' my nephew's days in the future. Ben Wauneka will be able to see his own grandchildren come into the world."

"Oh." Uncle Lakai must be a fortune-teller. Tory wished Ben had warned her. The man didn't seem odd in any other ways, though.

"*You* will find his salvation."

"Me? But I'm not a researcher. Does that mean you think one of the outside people I've contacted will know of someone who's working on a new cure?"

Uncle Lakai shook his head. "Not outside. You must never leave the land between the sacred four corners. The People need you."

"But…" The old man's words confused her with his strange rambling.

She cleared her throat and tried again. "I will do whatever I can for the People while I fulfill my obligation and complete my contract. And I'll try my best to locate someone with a cure for Ben before I go. But eventually I'll have to leave Dinetah. This is not my home. I'm not a part of a clan here. I don't belong."

The old man clucked his tongue. "Ben Wauneka's cure will come from here in Dinetah, a gift from the *Yei*. Do not deliberately be obscure with me, young woman doctor. Your only obligation will forever be to the Navajo and to the clan whose roof shelters you. Our Plant Tender would not have chosen you if this were not so."

She took a deep breath and gave up. "Okay. Thanks for…uh…telling me."

"I have more to tell. Two things are very important for you to know." He stopped talking and took another long sip of coffee.

Tory sat back, waiting. This ought to be interesting.

Finally, the old man closed his eyes and began to speak. "Long ago, before the days were counted by the rise of the sun but after the time when the Changing Woman had given us rules to live by," Uncle Lakai said in the singsong voice that reminded Tory of the old Irish legend tellers.

"A *hataalii* discovered a new dark wind and named it greed," he went on. "That medicine man joined with others to turn certain powers given to them for only good into something used for only evil.

"The evil *hataalii* was a very powerful and smart human," Uncle Lakai continued. "But he longed to become one of the *Yei*. Hidden in a cave under a river, this evil man discovered the powers of witchcraft. And soon he designed secret powders, made from sacred minerals and plants, that would give him superhuman strength. He went beyond nature to learn how to turn himself into animals who did not abide by the rules of Changing Woman."

As Lakai slowed down and took a drink, Tory almost interrupted him to ask a question. But something told her that would not be acceptable behavior. So she stayed quiet.

"Evil soon became the given name of that *hataalii*," he began again after a second breath. "Ancestors of the People also gave a name to the medicine men who had joined him in walking the earth in the skins of animals. Wherever their name was spoken, bad things befell the earth."

Uncle Lakai's voice lowered to a rasp. Tory almost stopped him and wondered if she should call someone to take him home. She worried that he was overtaxing himself.

He cleared his throat and shook his head, as if he knew of her fears and denied them. But his next sentences contained more Navajo words than English, and it became harder for Tory to keep up. He was obviously getting tired.

"The evil *hataalii* was not content to simply rule by greed. He envied the *Yei* their ability to have life never-ending. As he grew ever more powerful, he finally came upon their secret…." Old Uncle Lakai stopped speaking, but his blank ebony eyes had grown bright and danced with amusement in the glow of firelight.

"You don't mean that's where you're going to end the story," Tory grumbled without thinking.

Uncle Lakai reached a warm, bony hand over and patted hers. "Always leave part of the tale for others to finish. It is the Way."

"Yes, but…"

"There is one more thing that I must say now before I grow too tired. Shirley Nez has forgotten something that I have recently remembered."

Okay, now Tory really was confused. He'd completely changed topics again.

"Tell the Plant Tender she must search for the skunk-smelling raggedy goat sage. And to remember that it has other uses. She has forgotten them, and no one else knows the truth."

"All right. I'll give her the message. Now, let me find someone to come take you home." Tory jumped up, but then turned back when she remembered an important question that had been in the back of her mind. "Please, so that I may know how to ask someone to finish your tale, what do you call it? Does the legend have a name?"

"The story is one seldom told in public. Be careful who you ask.

"It goes by the name the People gave to the followers of the original evil *hataalii*," he added in a near whisper. "The ones who learned to change over and become animals. They still walk amongst us. Be careful of them."

Uncle Lakai's voice faded away and Tory stepped over to check on his welfare. As she leaned near, she could hear him mumbling under his breath and realized he'd almost fallen asleep. But she bent closer and listened anyway.

"Be careful, Plant Tender. They know you as you do not know them. Watch out for the…Skinwalkers."

Chapter 13

"**D**on't worry about the Navajo doctor," Shirley Nez told her with a shake of the head. "Ben Wauneka is safe in the company of the Brotherhood this afternoon. You must continue with your lessons. There isn't much time."

Tory checked her watch and then stared at the back of Shirley's head as the older woman headed up a narrow shale path toward what she'd called a special "collecting site."

"We have hours of daylight left," Tory called after her. She hurried to catch up as she gingerly picked her way through the loose rocks and sand. Her head already spinning with plant names and uses, Tory was still determined to learn every new lesson Shirley could teach.

She had on shorts while Shirley wore long slacks, but both sported wide-brimmed hats. Tory imagined herself looking like a lost Anglo tourist. Fortunately, her hat was made out of fashionable straw, while the odd-shaped thing sitting on Shirley's head seemed to be created from a light-gray felt and was incredibly misshapen and ugly.

The sun felt beyond hot up here at this altitude as the heat radiated off sandstone rocks and granite boulders. Shirley claimed they were going to a high place where the *hataaliis* regularly found sacred plants. But Tory wondered how any living thing could grow in such a harsh environment. This would be a good lesson for her to learn.

Without stopping, Shirley began speaking over her shoulder as she climbed the shale footholds. "We are moving through one of many drainages on the eastern slopes of the Chuska Mountain range. It's late spring now and the snow melt is mostly dried up. But notice the water seep starting to show up here and there?

"You've already visited the low grassy areas where the *hataaliis* gather plants for Enemy and Life Way ceremonies," Shirley continued as she climbed. "We are now searching for a much rarer plant that is very important to the heritage of the Dine."

The older woman stopped to take a breath. "It provided the People with much-needed moisture in ancient times of severe drought. But due to the modern ravages of strip coal mining and our water table being contaminated with uranium runoff, this Plant Clan has retreated and now hides in secret cliff dwellings."

"What is it used for these days if it's so rare?"

Shirley shook her head and took another step. "Only the *hataaliis* use it anymore, in their prayer sticks and for one or two special cures. They tell me it seems to make a patient's breathing come easier, but there are other cures more readily available for that."

They rounded a granite boulder and Tory was amazed to discover they were suddenly walking beside a real stream of water. Amazed because a minute ago she couldn't imagine a drier spot on the face of the earth except for either the Sahara or Gobi Desert.

Deep shadows began to dance eerily against the granite canyon walls. Looking like jumping sheep or goats, the shadows made her think of the message she had to deliver.

"By the way, Plant Tender," she called out to Shirley. "Hastiin Lakai Begay asked me to mention the skunk-smelling raggedy goat sage to you and to say that you should remember it has other uses."

"Did the elder say why he wanted me to think of it?"

Tory shook her head. "He seemed very concerned that you should remember that particular plant, though."

Shirley looked puzzled but turned and kept on climbing. "This stream flows year-round," she said after a few minutes of quiet. "And another couple of hundred feet up this canyon we will encounter a pleasant surprise."

The stream had already been a nice surprise as far as Tory was concerned. But while she kept up the pace behind Shirley, she spotted more and more plants growing beside the stream. Tory glanced ahead to where the canyon floor grew wider and spied what looked like a full-size pine tree.

"A pond?" Tory asked when she came close enough to see the crystal water surrounded by a few ponderosa pines.

"A mountain pool," Shirley answered. "But what we seek is farther upstream."

They passed the clear pool and Tory had a great deal of difficulty not jumping in. It looked so inviting. But then plants were growing everywhere beside the stream, and Shirley named each one as they walked by.

Moss and monkeyflowers lined the water as the canyon walls narrowed again and the spires of the cliffs rose higher above them, blocking out the sun. Finally, in one of the darkest crevices ahead Tory spotted a couple of tall, bushy plants with tiny white flowers and long, tangled roots.

"Oh," Shirley said with a groan that sounded like dismay. She came to an abrupt halt and put her hands on her hips.

"What's wrong?"

"Many of the plants have moved on." Shirley walked upstream a little more. "Look, here. The Plant Clan did not go on its own. Someone has dug up most of them. And whoever it was, they weren't careful how they went about taking them, either." Shirley knelt to check the ground around the deep holes, where something had obviously been removed.

Tory could tell that Shirley was shocked and upset. In fact, she'd never seen the woman so disturbed before.

"Do you think a *hataalii* came up here and took them without letting you know? Or maybe it was an animal on a digging rampage or something?" Tory was searching for answers that would calm the woman.

Shirley just kept shaking her head. "It's crazy. There's no reason anyone…"

Just then, from high above their heads, a long, desolate-sounding cry from a wild animal filled the canyon with echoes. Tory jumped nearly a foot in the air and when she came to earth, her adrenaline was pumping and she was ready to run for it.

"What the heck was that?"

Shirley stood, looked up and searched the rim of the canyon. "Look," she said with a deep frown.

Tory lifted her head and stared up to where the older

woman pointed. All of a sudden, one of the shadows actually moved and a pair of tall pointed ears came into view.

"It's a coyote, or a wolf, isn't it?" Tory stuttered.

"Look closer," Shirley told her.

After she'd swallowed back a spike of fear, Tory looked up again. This time, it was easier to see that the ears were attached to some kind of furry mask. It wasn't a real animal at all, but a man, standing about six feet tall and in disguise as a giant wolf.

Instead of being soothed by the knowledge that they weren't been stalked by a wild beast, Tory's sense of danger increased tenfold. "We have to get out of here." She grabbed Shirley's arm, turned and marched in double time downhill past the pool and lower on downward beside the creekbed.

"We cannot leave the Plant Clan," Shirley muttered as Tory dragged her along.

"Yes, we can. Someone wants us to leave and we're going—now."

For thirty minutes she pulled the older woman behind her as they traveled backwards the way they'd come. They moved beyond where they'd first seen the water in the creek. Then they climbed back down the shale footholds along the dry drainage bed.

Finally, sweating profusely and breathing heavily, the two of them arrived back where they had left Ben's SUV. Tory was a little hesitant to go near the vehicle. But after she'd checked it over and found it still locked and seeming the same as when they'd left, she hurried Shirley inside.

She locked the doors behind them, cranked the key in the ignition and let the air-conditioning blast them with heat-relieving chilled air. "I don't think anyone followed us. We should be okay now."

"We need to go back up there," Shirley muttered.

"Someone is stealing the Plant Clan and we have to stop them."

"Uh, I don't think so. We'll let the tribal police handle it. That guy looked deadly serious to me."

Shirley shook her head, buckled her seat belt and folded her arms over her chest.

"I have an idea." Tory dug under the seat for her carryall and pulled out the cell phone Ben had given her. "This is exactly the sort of time when I'm supposed to make a call to the Brotherhood."

"Yes," Shirley said with a nod of approval. "Something unnatural is happening here. This is information the Brotherhood will need."

Ben's eyesight was gone again by the time he and Hunter had driven up the canyon where Tory and Shirley were still parked in his SUV. It had taken so long to reach them that his every nerve ending was on edge.

He'd made Tory stay on the phone talking to him for the last half hour while he'd urged Hunter to race here. His heart pounded wildly, though several other members of the Brotherhood had arrived at least fifteen minutes ago, and he'd been assured that she and Shirley were fine. It had still soothed him to hear her voice over the phone.

The two women should never have been allowed to go out unescorted, he chided himself. Even in the daylight. What the hell had he been thinking?

He was out the door of Hunter's SUV before it came to a complete stop. Needing to touch Tory, he wanted to make sure by the static electricity they always shared whenever they came together that she was okay.

"Ben, you're not seeing again." Tory's voice sounded

shrill coming through the cell phone at his ear. "Stand still and keep a hand on the bumper. I'll be there in a second."

Damn his disease. Most of the time it didn't much matter. But there were times when not being able to see was the worst kind of hell.

He wanted to be her savior, not the other way around.

The zing of sensation as she reached his side and took his elbow told him everything was still all right. "Why didn't you call sooner?" he demanded with the annoyance plain in his voice.

"When? You mean up by the pool?" Tory sounded just as irritated by his question as he'd been asking it. "In the first place, we needed to get away from there as fast as possible and not stick around chatting on the phone. And in the second place, I didn't bring the cell with me up into the cliffs. I didn't figure it would get a signal in that narrow canyon and it was just one more thing not necessary to carry."

Drawing a deep breath and trying to calm down, Ben reached out and touched her cheek. He could feel the frown lines on her face and spent a moment tenderly stroking them away with his thumb. Soon he heard her breathing deepen, and felt her face relax under his fingertips.

"I'm sorry you were worried," she whispered at last. "I was pretty scared, too, for a while."

He was forced to clear his throat to speak. "If you and Shirley want to go out again, I think it would be wise for someone in the Brotherhood to accompany you to these remote areas."

"All the time? But why? I imagine we just stumbled on some illegal activity up there—like a drug hideout or drop-off or something. Shirley and I shouldn't need protection everywhere we go. We won't come back here, I guarantee."

Ben experienced a moment of panic. What reason could he give her for needing a guard? He couldn't tell her about the Skinwalker war. She would never understand.

Not totally sure himself why anyone would need protecting in such a remote canyon and in broad daylight, he turned to seek an answer before he gave one. "Is Shirley Nez nearby?"

"Yes, just a minute. She's talking to a couple of your cousins." He heard Tory call the Plant Tender over.

"Yes, *hataalii?*" Shirley said when she stood close.

He knew Tory was listening and he tried to hedge his words to keep her from thinking of more questions. "You said someone is stealing the Plant Clan. Taking them away by force. What plants are missing?"

"It was the Leaf Scar that someone dug up," Shirley told him. "The plants are now rare, but I still do not understand why anyone would be so desperate to have or destroy them."

"Leaf Scar? But that's…" It came to him then, the thing that had been niggling at the back of his mind. "Leaf Scar can also be found near Tocito Wash these days, isn't that right?"

"Yes. But that area was a little out of our range for today's lesson," Shirley answered. "Why do you mention it?"

"A patient of mine, along with her nephew, recently encountered someone in an arroyo near Tocito Wash that looked to them like the Navajo Wolf. I wonder now if that might not be related to this incident."

His own words rang a sound of alarm in his ears. "Will you two please wait in my SUV for a few minutes while I speak to my cousins?" he quickly urged. "And then, Tory, I think it would a great idea if you drove the three of us back to my office as soon as possible."

* * *

Tory's head was spinning again as she and Shirley waited for Ben in the air-conditioned SUV. This time the dizziness wasn't due to the plant names, but because of the many questions without adequate answers swirling through her brain.

She twisted under the steering wheel, rested her knee on the seat and turned her head to talk to Shirley, who was sitting in the backseat. There were a couple of things that she hoped Shirley would be able to tell her.

"Excuse me, Plant Tender. But could you please explain about the Navajo Wolf and tell me why anyone would dress up like one to scare people?"

"Hmm," Shirley murmured absently. "There is an old Dine legend you probably have not heard about evil and greed. And you should…"

"The Skinwalker legend, you mean? Hastiin Lakai Begay told me most of it the other night at the ceremony. Is the Navajo Wolf part of that story?"

Shirley stayed quiet for a couple of beats too long. Tory wasn't sure the other woman's silence was because the two stories of Skinwalkers and wolves were not the same—or because they were and it wasn't something an Anglo should mention.

Finally, Shirley began, "The elder Begay is correct that you must eventually know the Skinwalker story. But he should not have given you only some of the facts. It is dangerous for you to ask for answers on subjects so delicate."

"Dangerous? But they're only old legends. Why would that be dangerous?"

"I've heard Ben Wauneka ask in the past for you to keep an open mind to our ways. And I believe you have learned much from listening while I spoke of the Dine Way along with your plant lessons. Now again I ask that you accept what I say without letting your *bilagáana* background and superstitions interfere."

Her "white" superstitions? Wasn't that an interesting concept? But Tory kept her mouth firmly closed.

"The original evil one," Shirley began in a soft legend-teller voice, "the *first* Skinwalker, was not a story character but an actual man who taught himself and his followers how to turn into animals. The animal he picked for himself was the wolf, as he intended to remain the leader of his pack.

"What's more," Shirley added, "he knew most Navajo of the time were sheep and goat herders who would fear a wolf above all other animals."

Shirley's voice grew hoarse, but she kept on talking. "The Evil One promoted stories of terror that surrounded the Navajo Wolf, a supernatural entity who could get his way by using threats and magic. And eventually, just the name Skinwalker would cause mass panic. Even today, people refuse to speak the dreaded word for fear of retribution."

Taking a breath, Shirley stared out the window at the canyon's steep, barren slopes. "According to the rest of the legend seldom told, the original Navajo Wolf had indeed uncovered the secret to longevity. He ruled the Dine by terror for over a thousand years.

"When the evil master was finally near death, he buried most of his secrets, allowing only one man per generation the knowledge of how to become the Navajo Wolf."

"So supposedly there is a modern man somewhere in Dinetah who can actually turn himself into the Navajo Wolf?" Tory asked incredulously.

"Not supposedly. I know it to be a fact."

"But that…that Halloween character we saw up in the canyon was a real man and not a wolf. I doubt if there was anything superhuman about him, either."

"Yes, that is so," Shirley agreed. "Throughout the centuries, each man who carries the secret has recruited others to join in his evil-doings. Each Navajo Wolf teaches his men how to become other types of unnatural beings. Snakes, birds, dogs. Some are traditional allies of the Wolf, others newly turned to the dark wind.

"They mostly terrorize the remote and uneducated Dine," Shirley went on. "Their goals are control of the land, minerals or water. It's all based on greed, which is an opposing morality to the Navajo Way."

"So this is some kind of secret society? Or cult? Like the teenagers became involved with?"

"Yes, though I know of many cases where evil men who have no real connection will impersonate Skinwalkers in order to capitalize on the terror and get what they want through fear. I would say that is what our 'Wolf' stalker was attempting today. I just still don't understand why."

This woman could not possibly believe what she was saying. Could she?

Tory scraped a hand over her face and tried to think. If the story were really true, wouldn't the rest of the world know about it? It would've shown up in scientific journals, or at the very least on *Ripley's Believe It or Not.*

She respected Shirley Nez and had begun to think of her as more than just a teacher. There had to be a way of reconciling the Wolf story to her growing friendship with a woman who seemed so intelligent.

Just then, Hunter Long brought Ben back to the SUV and it was time to go. Good thing. Tory needed more time to think through the Navajo Wolf story. Maybe a lot more time.

Ben sat quietly as Tory drove them all back to his mesa. He could tell by the tension in the air that something had happened, but he wasn't sure how bad it might be. Shirley seemed too quiet sitting in the backseat, and Tory might as well have been a stone beside him.

This was one of those times when seeing Tory's expression would've been worth a thousand words.

After a while he heard his transmission wheezing under the assault of climbing the road nearest his house. In a few minutes they would all be freed from the captivity of riding in this SUV. Maybe things would get better then.

"I heard an odd rumor from one of my old professors a few weeks ago," Tory said. "And I've been sitting here wondering what sort of logical reason anyone might have for taking plants and then guarding the empty spot. It would have to be something involving a great deal of money for anyone to go to such trouble, don't you think?"

"Yeah," he agreed, but then wondered where she was going with this.

"Well, my med school pharmacology professor heard through his connections that there's a nongovernmental drug development lab located on the Navajo reservation. And that the lab has quietly been doing research on cancer cures. Either of you ever heard of such a thing?"

Ben and Shirley Nez answered in unison. "No."

Shirley got her question out before Ben could formulate the question on his tongue. "Wouldn't a lab like that take huge amounts of money to put together?" she asked.

"Hundreds of thousands just to buy the equipment," Tory replied. "Not to mention salaries for the researchers, and probably a ton more cash just to keep things secret. I thought *that* much money might qualify as enough to make someone do seemingly crazy things—like stealing plants."

"I agree," he said. "Do you think you can help us find

out more about this lab—or perhaps about the exact kind of research they've been doing?"

"I can try," Tory told him.

He heard her downshift for the final pull into his yard just as an inappropriate grin broke out across his face. Every time she did or said something like this it made him want to smile.

Dr. Tory Sommer was just too damn smart for her own good. And he loved her for it.

Chapter 14

Shirley Nez sat cross-legged on the floor of her ceremonial hogan. All alone, she chanted and prayed for guidance from the *Yei*.

Her premonitions were quite clear now and she had come to accept that her time was running out. There was much to do to prepare—papers, plans and maps to assemble for the new Plant Tender's use. All must be in place for the inevitable.

The new Plant Tender was not yet convinced of her calling. But Shirley knew such hesitation would not stop the dedicated *bilagáana* doctor from fulfilling her destiny.

Shirley Nez peered through the haze of time and had seen the future. But some small fact, some long-forgotten knowledge from the deep recesses of her memory, teased her—just out of reach.

It had to do with old Lakai Begay's reminder. The

skunk-smelling raggedy goat sage. She hadn't thought of that plant in a long time. It made a wonderful tea, terrific for curing excess stomach acid as she remembered.

But that particular Plant Clan had not been seen in Dinetah for many years. While Shirley gathered together her old maps and lists for the new Plant Tender, she tried to think of where the goat sage might have relocated.

Thoughts of the ancient, sacred plant and of what her grandmother had taught her of its uses stayed just below the surface of Shirley's mind as she went about the business of preparing to meet the *Yei*. There was something of vast importance that Hastiin Lakai Begay had been trying to tell her. It would be no use asking him for clarification, however; the elder would only remind her that it was the Plant Tender's job to know the whereabouts and uses of the Plant Clan. In that, he was correct.

But there *was* some other curative power that sage possessed—and an urgent reason for finding it—she felt positive. Her duty as Plant Tender for the *hataalii* meant she must remember what it was before her time between the four sacred mountains completely ran out.

It had been five days since the Wolf incident, but Tory hadn't had five minutes to consider the ramifications and possibilities of the Skinwalker story. She and Ben had been treating a rash of summer colds, babies with ear infections and an amazing array of sprained ankles and various work-related cuts and scrapes.

Even now, as she and Ben sought frantically to help a young girl who was having an asthma attack, her mind wandered. She wanted a second to check her e-mail for word on cancer cures coming out of a Navajo drug-research lab.

During every odd break in the action since that day in

the canyon. she would dash back to Ben's office to use his online computer. She'd contacted friends—and friends of friends—anyone who might have some information about the apparently secret lab on the rez.

Over the last few days, Ben's illness appeared to have reached a tentative plateau. In daylight he saw well enough to get around and to treat patients without them guessing he was losing his eyesight. But after sundown he always fell into a deep hole of total blackness where he couldn't see a thing

In an effort to make his nights pass more quickly, Shirley Nez had brought over plant lists and maps by the armful so Tory and Ben could work together on her studies. And so Tory would not have to leave him when he needed her the most. He would think of a particular plant and she would recite its uses and its last known whereabouts in Dinetah.

It seemed like a game, one only a *hataalii* could play. And soon they both looked forward to their time alone after dinner.

But Tory also dreaded those quiet times. Worried each night about the unfamiliar warmth and companionship they shared. And secretly hated that they continued to retreat to separate rooms when it came time to sleep.

She'd tried so hard to be careful with her heart. The lust and love she felt for Ben had been packed away—well, at least it was kept out of sight.

Yet every time she heard his deep laugh or listened to him praise her efforts with the plant names, the heart of the child she'd once been pounded threateningly in her chest.

The heart of that scared little girl—the one who had watched her daddy die and seen her safety net go down on the living-room floor in front of her eyes—longed for an opportunity to find a cure for Ben as she wasn't able to for her father. Her head hurt from memorizing plants and cures. But with every new plant, a tiny niggle of hope sprouted in her chest.

By now she had completely accepted the concept of alternative cures. So many of them worked for Ben's patients. And these last few days on the computer she'd read enough about new rediscoveries of ancient plant cures from the rain forests and deserts of the world that she had become a true disciple of the possibilities.

So, during the day she stayed busy and during the night she learned to recognize the Plant Clan while keeping Ben's spirits up at the same time. Even the earliest hours of prelight were filled, as Ben said dawn chants and she sneaked out to his garden to check on the plants and water them.

Most of the nights when she fell into bed, she immediately dropped into a black, dreamless sleep. But last night she'd dreamed *that* dream again. The one of Ben carrying her up the side of a cliff while something horrible chased at their heels.

She'd originally thought that dream was a warning about the landslide they had survived. Now she wondered if its meaning had more to do with the yellow, gleaming eyes and sharp fangs of the wolf that had been after them.

Just the idea of a *real* Navajo Wolf made her shiver in the heat of the examining room.

Ben had the AC off, trying to help the asthmatic girl's breathing by using both a nebulizer the girl didn't like and by running an old-fashioned vaporizer filled with a special concoction he'd made using plant remedies.

While Tory administered drug therapies by injection, Ben kept up a steady chant and searched through his dried herbs and leaves for other possible cures to add to his breathing treatment.

"Ah," he mumbled absently when he found a bottle of some dried plant way in the back of one of his herb shelves. "I remember. Son of a..."

Tory looked over at him for clarification of what he'd meant by that. But he gave her a slight shake of the head, as if to say he didn't want to talk about it in front of the patient and her frightened mother.

He turned to the child and smiled, in that gentle, authoritative way he had. "I have the exact right thing to cure the dark wind that has seized you," he told her.

Adding the dried leaves to the vaporizer's water, Ben's whole body held such an air of competence that even Tory was breathing easier. And in just a few minutes, so was the little girl.

It didn't much matter whether the drugs, the vaporizer or Ben's supreme confidence had turned the tide. The emergency was over for now.

While the mother thanked Ben, the little girl giggled and Tory searched out medicines and inhalers for them to take home with them, her treacherous heart failed her.

She loved him—damn it.

More and more with every passing minute. There was no cure, no white man's drug nor Navajo remedy for the disease that ailed her. What in heaven's name would she do when her contract on the rez was complete and they sent her away?

Willing the pain back into the hidden box in her heart where she tried to keep it buried, Tory filled out the patient's charts and cleaned up the examining room. She zipped back to the computer and checked her e-mail while Ben saw the mother and daughter off in their old pickup truck.

Ten minutes later Tory opened the outside door and pushed back the blanket to find Ben sitting quietly on the bench beside the entryway. "Are you okay? How's your vision?"

"Still blurry, but I can see well enough," he replied. "Sit with me a moment?"

She sat beside him, but was careful not to let their bodies touch. It was difficult being this close and not being able to throw her arms around him.

"Before," he began. "When I found the bottle of dried Leaf Scar to help that child's breathing, the old rumors and speculations came back to me with unfortunate clarity."

"What? Why unfortunate?"

"I remembered my great-grandfather, who was a very well-respected medicine man, giving me lessons on plant remedies and the Dine Way when I was a boy. He told me of a rumor that had been spread off the reservation by some city Navajos that a cure for lung cancer was secretly being kept from the rest of the world by the eldest *hataaliis*."

"Lung cancer? Wow. Was it true?"

"No, certainly not. The Dine would not deliberately keep such a boon to world health a secret. But…"

"But?"

"Changing Woman gifted the People with many special blessings. Some of them are only meant to be used on the land between the four sacred mountains—the land of the Dine. A few of the more complex cures you have been studying should not be shared openly off the reservation."

"Why not? If they work here, won't they work everywhere?"

"Perhaps. But the problem is that many of the plants will not grow anywhere else. And synthesizing them has proven for the most part impossible. It's been tried. All the so-called experts succeeded in doing was to ruin our plant habitat and bring false hopes to suffering people.

"That's what happened to the Leaf Scar," he continued. "Why it has retreated to hide in difficult-to-reach, remote places in Dinetah. It was the main ingredient in this supposed lung cancer cure."

"And now, someone has once again brought up the rumor and is stealing the few remaining plants?"

He nodded. "Looks that way."

Tory tried to absorb what he'd told her. She understood about dashed hopes and had learned early in her life about charlatans.

"Well, that might help us," she finally managed to say. "Now we know it's supposedly a lung cancer drug treatment and we know the lab is probably not legitimate. All I have to do is put that bug in the right ear and I should start getting a lot of information."

"No."

"Huh? I thought you wanted my help."

"I changed my mind. It could be dangerous for you. Think again of how much money must be involved. And now that I've remembered what happened the last time, I also remember my grandfather telling me that the *hataaliis* of the day had gone to great lengths to hush up the rumors. They wiped out any trace of anything to do with those false cures."

"So someone else has dug up the information somehow and is smart enough and devious enough to use it. How could that be dangerous for me?"

"That *someone* has to be a person with connections on the rez. Old connections. And perhaps…" He let his thought drag out until, with a shake of his head, he began again.

"The Brotherhood will take over from here. Let them handle it."

The Brotherhood again. Why did the whole idea of such an organization suddenly sound strange to her? Even with all the safety promises, slogans and lectures she'd gotten about them, the group's image just reeked of vigilantism.

At that precise moment, Kody Long's truck pulled up the drive to Ben's office. More than vigilantes, there was a kind of mysticism that swirled around these guys. It was as if you could just think the name Brotherhood and they would show up. Weird.

"Ya'at'eeh," Kody said as he stepped from the truck.

"Ya'at'eeh, cousin," Ben responded.

Tory waved a limp-wristed hand, totally unimpressed by the ritual this afternoon.

She did have enough sense to wait until some of the normal pleasantries were completed before she jumped feet first into her questions.

"Do you have any news for us?" she demanded of Kody when there was a lull. "The last we heard, the Brotherhood was rounding up the bad guys and were trying to figure out who the 'hotshot medicine dude' might be. Oh, and have the FBI or the police got Coach Singleton in custody yet?"

Kody stood before them, hands on hips, and gave her a wry grin. "You're tougher than the Bureau's best interrogators, Doc.

"There is some news," he continued, growing more sober. "But things are not happening as quickly as any of us would like. We've managed to locate all but a couple of the teens who belonged to that cult. They are going through deprogramming as we speak. But Coach Singleton has eluded us so far, and no one has been able to identify the supposed 'hotshot medicine dude,' either."

Kody turned his head slightly to address Ben. "Are your eyes seeing light or dark today, cuz?"

"I have unfortunately become accustomed to hazy yellow in the afternoons. Why?"

"We got a tip that Coach Singleton has had some kind of dealings with the Plant Clan thieves. And that he may be hiding out in a cabin up near the Tocito Wash area. We'd like for you to go with us as we check out the rumor. Is that a possibility today?"

Tory wanted to be heard before Ben answered. "It sounds dangerous. Why do you need Ben?"

Kody tried to hide a deepening grin. "Your mentor has developed a sort of sixth sense. We have a young man in our custody who claims he was never under the influence of the drugs but knows a lot about the cult. He promised to guide us to the cabin. But we would prefer not walking into a trap, so we hoped that Ben could listen and dig out any falsehoods in the boy's statements."

"Lucas Tso is much better than I am at such things," Ben broke in

"Our cousin the artist has temporarily left the sacred lands. He's preparing for a grand art exhibit in Sante Fe next week."

"Hmm," Ben muttered. "I don't like the idea of leaving…."

"If I can go along to help Ben get around then it should be okay," Tory broke in to agree graciously.

"No," both men said as one.

"I've asked Shirley Nez to come by here this afternoon and stay the night with you," Kody told her. "The Brotherhood is capable of helping Ben with his movements. And we'll all feel much less stress if we can be sure you're safe at home."

"But—"

Ben reached over and took her hands with both of his. "Do not worry, tigress. Your cub will return safe and sound." He squeezed her hands with a firm but gentle grip. "I'm grateful that you're concerned about my welfare. But don't be. I have to learn to do these sorts of things for myself, Tory. You won't always be around to guide my way."

Oh, hell. He would have to go and say something like that. Irritation, despair, and a silent longing so deep it seemed to come from childhood all conspired to keep her quiet and to reluctantly accept his decision.

Fine. She would stay here with Shirley this evening. But she would be damned if she was going to stay off the Internet. She had decided it was her duty to find out everything she possibly could about the phony research lab.

It was the least she could do to help.

"How is married life, and are things okay with your new wife?" Ben couldn't turn his thoughts away from Tory, so he tried to make small talk with Kody as they drove through the magenta sunset to meet the Brotherhood near Tocito Wash.

"Reagan's fine, thanks," Kody said with a smile. "Growing big as a house with our child and irritated as hell that she's stuck more and more inside by the computer."

"She's decided she likes it here in Dinetah? I know when Reagan first came she had some reservations— Uh...no pun intended."

Kody barked out a laugh and downshifted to take the next grade. "It wasn't Dinetah that concerned her. When

Reagan first showed up on the rez, she didn't know a soul and had never spent much time outdoors. Top that off with the fact that Skinwalkers were trying to control her mind, and no one could blame her for 'having reservations.'"

Ben let the grin spread over his face as he appreciated his cousin's Navajo-style wry humor. Then he sat back and tried to enjoy the view. There might not be many more times when he would be able to see a sunset over the cliffs and mesas of his homeland.

But he knew there were questions he should be asking, difficult questions. "Tell me what you were hiding from Tory back there. What do we know?"

"See? You are getting as good at this as Lucas Tso."

Ben crossed his arms over his chest and scowled. "I didn't need to be a mind reader to know that."

Kody nodded sharply and his eyes narrowed. "We're positive now that Coach Singleton has joined the Skinwalkers. One of the cult recruits we rescued swears he saw the man turn himself into a bird and fly away."

"Was it a raven, by any chance?"

Shrugging, Kody went on, "Kid was too damned scared to notice. Not sure he would've been able to determine the species, anyway. You know these kids are more into video games and cool clothes than they are the old Dine Ways that their parents took for granted."

"So, the Brotherhood has concluded then that the plant thieves are probably Skinwalkers, too," Ben remarked. "I've remembered an old story my grandfather told about the Leaf Scar being used by a Skinwalker to deal a public blow against the *hataaliis* back in the fifties. Someone swore to the white medical establishment that Leaf Scar cured lung cancer and that the medicine men had known it but refused to share the knowledge with the world."

"You think this new Skinwalker society is using the same old scam?"

"The same scam, different group, different reason. From what I've seen, this new incarnation of Skinwalkers is all about money. And they are much smarter and more widespread than any of their previous generations of evil.

"I don't think they feel terribly threatened by the *hataaliis*," Ben continued. "Because these particular evil ones are out to control the world, not just superstitious Navajos."

Ben took a breath and qualified his own statement. "The Brotherhood may be a somewhat different story for the Skinwalkers than the elder *hataaliis* are, as we've actually slowed this group down on occasion. But still, I'm guessing what the Skinwalkers want the most is more money. Probably provided by the wealthy world drug manufacturers this time."

Kody nodded. "Now that we have a direction, Reagan can locate the 'who' and the 'where.'"

"Tell your wife to do nothing that would lead anyone back to her. It could be extremely dangerous."

"Reagan? You're kidding. You know she can get any information whenever she wants about whoever she wants. And without a soul ever knowing who was looking for the info. My FBI superiors would love to be able to get into as many secure places as she does without a warrant. Reagan has…uh…her ways…and her contacts." Kody chuckled.

Ben would've smiled but the situation was too serious. "What else have you not yet said? Have we narrowed the list in order to find the person in medicine we've heard about?"

"Some," Kody answered. "Reagan has discovered

dozens, maybe hundreds, of e-mail messages coming and going from the Raven Wash Clinic. She hasn't been able to hack into all of the messages yet, but a couple of them were sent out by someone calling themselves 'the Raven.'"

"Raven Wash," Ben muttered absently. "That still leaves several possible suspects. There's maybe half a dozen guys there that could be called 'that medicine dude.'"

"Judging by the sheer volume of messages," Kody told him, "I'd say that the person we seek must have pretty unlimited access to the computer system there. That should help narrow it down at least a little."

Just who the Raven might be was something for Ben to consider as they continued driving along Navajo Route 9 to meet up with the other members of the Brotherhood. Maybe tonight they would be able to capture one of the Skinwalkers and then make him tell what he knew of the rest of the society.

If Ben hadn't been so occupied with thoughts of Tory, however, he would've known better than to yearn for something he knew deep down was totally impossible.

Chapter 15

Worn out, but more emotionally despondent than physically, Ben returned to his home shortly after dawn the next morning.

The night's battle with the Skinwalkers had seemed particularly brutal to him. Perhaps it was because when his eyes went blind, his other senses became so much more acute. Distant cries of anguish and pain rang in his ears. The smell of death clung to his clothes and skin. The flavor of blood sent metallic tastes to sour his stomach.

He had so hoped that no one would be injured, and that the Brotherhood would be able to take a Skinwalker warrior alive. Instead, it was just another bad joke on them all. They had actually captured one of the evil ones. They took Coach Singleton alive in his human form, though the other young men witches had slipped away into the night.

But before any of the Brotherhood could finish saying

the chants that would weaken the coach enough to ask their questions, he'd turned himself into a vulture and attacked with his superhuman strength.

He'd given them no choice but to shoot down the bird.

Ben had said prayers over the remains of the unearthly being. And while he did, he'd prayed as he had many times before that the Brotherhood would somehow uncover an ancient chant or potion that would paralyze a Skinwalker. He longed to be able to turn them forever away from the dark wind so they could return to the living and their clans and families.

There were old rumors and whispers that such magical chants and potions had existed once in Dinetah. The elder *hataaliis* all told tales of how a single good medicine man with the right chant had been the one to bring down the original Skinwalker after his thousand-year reign of terror.

Ben knew his cousin Michael Ayze was spending all his spare hours searching ancient ruins and hidden archeological sites for any sign of such a chant or potion. If a thing like that had ever existed in Dinetah, they must find it again. Or the Skinwalker power would eventually overwhelm them all.

With his heart heavy and his vision nearly clear in the growing daylight, Ben climbed the stairs to his front deck. Before he went inside, it occurred to him that Tory might still be sleeping on his sofa in the front room. He turned and walked around the side of the house toward the medicine hogan, hoping not to disturb her.

But when he rounded the last corner of the house, he stopped in his tracks and stared at the old cottonwood tree that stood at the edge of his garden and partially shaded the front of the medicine hogan. He beheld a sight that put a zing back in his body and erased the black spirits from his mind.

There, on a double-wide swing that had never existed before, sat the most beautiful woman he had ever seen. Tory, with her blond hair streaming down her back, her long cotton T-shirt blowing in the breeze and her bare feet and legs pumping her higher and higher into the air.

Had she built the swing all on her own? Or perhaps a Skinwalker had conjured it up to tempt him.

His feet propelled him toward the vision. "Good morning," he said softly in English. "Where'd you get the swing?"

She looked over at him and for a split second he caught emotions hiding in her gray-blue eyes that he didn't recognize. But then…the mere sight of her began to caress his spirits, sending his libido into a spin and liquefying his granite heart.

Masking whatever feelings had been in her eyes, Tory smiled at him. Using her feet as brakes, she brought the wide-seated swing to a stop.

"Shirley Nez brought it and I helped her set it up yesterday afternoon," she told him with a sad smile in her voice. "She just left, by the way. Said to tell you the swing is to keep your youngest patients occupied while they wait to see you."

"May I join you?" His heart was pounding at the thought of sitting next to her, and he hoped she wouldn't notice and laugh at him.

"Sure," she said as she scooted over. "It's so peaceful out here at this early hour. I just love being able to look over the entire garden. It seems like you can watch the plants growing."

The juxtaposition of last night's horror contrasted sharply with the sweetness of Tory's smile. It made him catch his breath. The tender sight of her sent him rolling backward into urgent longings he had tried to bury.

The only thing he wanted now, would ever want, was to lose himself with her. To forget everything else—wars, vows, traditions, blindness—everything.

He sat beside her, but not touching. "Let's just sit and enjoy the quiet for a few minutes. I don't think I'm quite ready for swinging."

She murmured her agreement, and the sound was low and sensual in her throat. Ben gripped the swing's rope and gritted his teeth, struggling hard for control.

Every night since she'd been staying with him, he'd lain awake in bed and ached for her. Ached to walk the few feet out to his great-room sofa. Ached to take her in his arms.

His big, comfortable bed had never seemed so lonely.

There were so many bad reasons for the two of them to come together physically. And so many good reasons for them not to.

But this celibate thing had gone way too far. Kody Long had been every bit as virile and strong in last night's battle as any of the bachelor members of the Brotherhood who swore they were remaining celibate and sticking with their vows. Yet Kody got to go home to climb into a warm bed with his beautiful wife last night, the same as he did every night.

Ben remembered he hadn't felt the least bit...under-powered after his one night with Tory. If anything, he had been stronger and sharper than ever before.

No. He would tell the Brotherhood that they need not keep their vows any longer. He didn't intend to himself. Perhaps the old legends had been just old wives' tales, anyway.

Tory fidgeted quietly next to him.

"What's that you have on?" he asked, afraid to really turn his attention to her and find out.

"This?" She looked down at herself and apparently just

then realized what she was wearing. "Oh. Well, this is what I wear for a nightshirt. You aren't supposed to see me in this old T-shirt thing. I thought I'd get a chance to shower and change before you came home."

"Sorry. But I'm not blind. Not at the moment, at least." But actually, he wished he was. Seeing her in the ultrasoft cotton shirt that probably stopped at midthigh was a temptation he could've done without.

And now he couldn't do anything except wonder what the hell she had on under it.

She sighed, and her chest raised and lowered with the deep breath. It made him want to chant, to pray, to do anything to get his mind off the fact that she obviously didn't have on a bra.

He needed her. Not just for sex, though that was a big part of it. And not just for help with his practice, though he couldn't have gone this far without her.

It was more along the lines that he just—needed her close. In a primal, fundamental kind of way. The exact way that Changing Woman had taught a man and a woman should be joined.

Barely caring at all anymore how long they had left to be together, Ben wondered if perhaps he should spend the rest of the day trying to explain his change of heart. Would she listen? Would she bless him by coming to his bed?

After all, he was sure that she wanted him—actually, it was more that she needed him as he needed her. That was what he'd seen in her eyes a minute ago.

Ben refused to allow himself to think of the other emotions he'd also seen there. The more tender, life-altering emotions he couldn't name and didn't want to accept.

Tory fidgeted beside him again, and he turned to see if he was crowding her.

Both of her hands were raised to the back of her head, which only succeeded in pushing her breasts even higher and more forward than they were before. The blood stopped running to his brain and time stood on its head as he held his breath.

"What's…" he croaked. Clearing his throat, he tried again. "What are you doing with your hair?"

"It's a wreck. I hadn't realized how long it had gotten in the time I've been working out here with you. I'm trying to put it up into a ponytail, just to get it off my neck."

The world tilted out of balance, and he knew the *Yei* had given him another chance to have what he so desired. To put back the balance between them.

"I'm pretty good when it comes to braiding hair. May I help?"

He saw her holding her breath, too, as she slowly turned to stare up at him. There it was again, buried in those mesmerizing gray-blues. The need. The desire.

He thanked whatever god had smiled on him for giving him the opportunity to see those eyes and feel that warm emotion one more time.

"Please do," she said hesitantly.

He didn't have to be asked twice. Scooping her up by the waist, he dragged her hips over his thigh and settled her bottom in between his legs with her back to him.

She hiccupped her surprise at his quick movements, but then steadied herself by grabbing hold of his knees and nesting her bottom between them to be more comfortable. The chance to fill his hands with her hair, with her, made his whole body shake in anticipation.

Finally, he wiped the sweat from his palms on his pants

leg, picked up a few sunshine-colored strands and let them slide slowly through his fingers. Spun gold. Satin temptation.

The sudden adrenaline surge nearly blew the top off his head, as testosterone splashed through his veins. For a few seconds he just sat there, with both his hands fisted in her hair, and experienced the tension as it built in his every nerve ending.

He let his eyes take in the gentle curve of her neck, the fine strands below her hairline. Desperate to remember all of the senses of her, he focused on the color, the texture.

Unable to resist, he bent his head and placed his lips against the tender skin on the side of her neck. Sweet and salty, his tongue delighted in the experience of Tory.

She took a breath, then leaned back against his chest with a moan. He dropped his hands and ran them lightly up and down her arms, loving how she felt as she trembled beneath his fingers.

But his hands seemed to be developing a mind of their own and came to the decision that they needed more. More of the feel of her. Something more to remember on all those lonely dark nights without her to come.

Sliding his hands around her rib cage, he gave his palms permission to fill themselves with her breasts. As they did, she made a funny little noise in the back of her throat. He felt her nipples harden beneath his hands, peaking and straining against the soft material.

Tory couldn't stand it. Couldn't stand all the tension coiling inside her. She had to touch. Had to see.

She took a breath, slid out from under his hands and flipped her body around, tucking her knees beside his thick, masculine thighs. When she looked into his eyes, she found them filled with promise—and confusion. Those emotions had been what she'd longed to see. He did want her, even though he was still conflicted by his own blatant sexual urges.

Good. So was she.

An early-morning breeze caught the ends of her hair and blew a few strands over her shoulders. It made her flash back to their one erotic night and the sensual pleasure of his long, loose hair floating across her neck, arms and chest as he moved down her body.

She tried to soak up his current image as he continued to watch her intently. That he could see her at all was more than thrilling. Something to savor in the long lonely years ahead without him.

All the while, as they sat there silently gazing at one another, soft cedar-scented gusts whispered at her back. The obvious hunger in those treacherous eyes of his was compelling. What woman wouldn't melt when the man she loved beyond redemption looked at her as though he might die if he couldn't touch, or couldn't watch her reactions as he did.

His hair was falling loose from its leather tether, and she reached up to brush a strand off his cheek. He never blinked at her movement. But when he shifted those deep sexy brown eyes to her neck and then lower, the skin under his glance began to flame.

Using the pad of his thumb, he gently stroked her skin directly above where she'd felt the fire. But that only succeeded in stoking the heat and driving it lower. In an instant she felt fully aroused.

If he didn't want to finish this, right here—right now—it would kill her. For it was far too late to stop. She tipped her head back and held his gaze, until she realized she'd been holding her breath.

As she filled her lungs with the crisp mountain air, she moved her own thumb over his strong, jutting chin. Letting her hands glide downward from there, she ran them over his Adam's apple and down to the base of his neck. Her body ached, felt as though fire ants crawled in her veins. Every tightly strung nerve begged her to go faster.

Smoothing her hands down his chest, she let them race across his shirt as they moved lower still. Pausing only long enough to flip open buttons with her nail, she was headed toward the belt buckle of his jeans.

Ben gritted his teeth and sat perfectly still. It had been quite stunning, that flush of hunger on his beloved's face as she stared up into his eyes. Her lips had parted as she watched him—and wanted.

Unwilling to resist the heated female invitation in her eyes, he cupped his hand behind her neck and pulled her sweet mouth into a kiss. She stroked his bottom lip with her tongue and his brain went south.

He took possession of her mouth. Slow and teasing at first, their kiss soon became deeper, ravenous and stunningly intense. As their tongues telegraphed sexual intent, his every nerve ending focused on her taste. Spun honey and spring sage.

Wet and carnal now, she was wild—and unbearably beautiful. He fought back a sheen of tears and let her take the lead.

It took a lot of well-focused Navajo endurance for him to sit there, continuing to kiss her as she ran her hand down to his jeans. When she laid a heavy palm over the hard ridge of his flesh beneath the zipper, he had to break their lips apart slightly to let out a gasp.

She hummed, licked her lips and dropped her chin to watch where her fingers where leading. He let her explore and nearly bit his tongue in two as she slowly, carefully undid the zipper and slipped her hands inside.

Making a low guttural hiss, the sound of both frustration and pleasure, he ripped the T-shirt up over her head and let his own hands roam freely across her naked body. He hadn't meant for things to go so far while they were still exposed and outside this way.

But their ragged breaths, as each gulped in air, told him there would be no backing down now.

With slow, tantalizing care, she released his erection from the prison of his jeans. He ground his mouth hard against hers, hungrily demanding the world—the whole world of her—while she calmly, coolly, flicked her finger over his moist tip straining between them.

When she curled her hand around his full length and stroked upward, his whole body jerked. No more control left, he grabbed her wrist and removed her hand from his pulsing flesh.

"Watch my eyes," he urged her. "Watch your own reflection there. You're so beautiful. Stay focused on me—with me."

Her eyes, glazed and dilated, locked to his.

In seconds, their breathing turned even more erratic. Both their pupils were wide and black with erotic intent, but still they remained frozen and stared into each other's eyes.

A desperate tinge at last moved into hers. She gripped his forearms, but continued trying to hold his gaze.

She shifted ever so slightly and he took the opportunity to slip his hands under her buttocks. Filling his hands with soft flesh, he helped as she lifted up and eased him right inside her body. She wrapped her legs around his waist and arched her back, driving him to the hilt.

He thrust against her once, on a long, shaky breath. With one sharp gasp, she arched again and he felt himself go even deeper.

They met each other then, movement for movement. With impeccable timing and perfectly in tune.

He held her, tight and secure, as the swing began to sway under their movements and each drive sent shattering splinters of desire to the base of his spine. Every sway brought both of them to the very brink of release. They climbed and crawled as one, moving through suspended time toward that edge. But before they could reach the peak, the swing would go back the other way, sending them spiraling out of control on an outgoing tide of erotic sensation.

It was an exquisite strain, holding himself steady inside her body's tight, wet embrace. They both made incoherent sounds, swearing into the morning breeze—savage, feral notes, they were the music of man and woman mating.

Still, as her body finally closed around him and pulsed her orgasm into them both, the blinding sensation of losing himself to her felt like coming home. A home that felt so right, yet seemed so foreign, it drove the air right out of his lungs. He was left feeling only the hot, molten lava of release, flowing through his arteries.

She collapsed against his chest, and he felt a rush of tenderness quite unlike anything he'd experienced before.

Running his hand up and down her back, he held himself immobile and listened to their combined heartbeats, stamping together to a savage drumbeat. He curled his fingers in her hair and hung on.

Body to body. Heat to heat. Heart to heart.

Tory wasn't sure she would ever be able to catch her breath again. Being with him this way was more...more than she could've hoped. More than she thought she could successfully handle and still live through, if and when he turned her away and backed off again.

How had she let herself in for so much more pain? Her first marriage was the better way to go as far as she was concerned. No pain. And definitely no strain when they parted.

How could she let herself forget what he thought of them? That she was an uptight Anglo who would leave the rez as soon as her contract was up, while he was a Navajo crystal gazer who was out to save his People by following old traditions.

But they fit. Damn it. Couldn't he tell how well they fit?

"You okay?" he whispered into her hair.

She pushed against his biceps and leaned back. It shocked her to see how his expression was showing his every emotion. The man was usually so staid.

But as he looked at her, she saw the wetness ringing his gentle eyes, while tiny teardrops still clung to his lashes. He stared at her with such tenderness in his gaze that it nearly brought tears to her own eyes. But she never cried.

"I'm fine," she said as she lifted herself off his lap. "Uh, *better* than fine. But I think we'd better go inside the house. I don't imagine anyone is around, but I'd hate for a patient to drive up while we were out here like this."

He helped to steady her before he stood and straightened his clothes. She looked around a second, located her T-shirt and quickly pulled it over her head. Coming out here in just a nightshirt had been a really stupid move.

And thank God she'd made it. No matter what pain might follow, she never would've wanted to miss this… this swing dance with a perfect lover.

Suddenly taking her hand, Ben forced her to stand still

and focus on his face. "I don't know how much more time I might have before I'm totally and irrevocably blind," he began gently. "And I'm not sure what my life will become when that happens. But until then, stay with me. Be one with me. Help me through the long nights as you have helped me through the darkening days."

Oh, hell. There was no hope at all for her now.

Pain be damned. No woman in her right mind would turn down an offer like that.

Obviously, she was not in her right mind or she wouldn't have let this whole relationship get started in the first place.

"Yes," she said and reached up to touch his cheek. "Yes, I'll stay with you. Be with you. You only have to make room in your life and in your bed, and I'm there."

Now and for always, she whispered silently in her head. As long as you will have me.

Chapter 16

The Raven sat back in his chair and threw his glasses on the desk. His gut was telling him things had gone out of control. The danger seemed to be closing in from all sides.

Someone was meddling in the Navajo Wolf's deal with the pharmaceutical company. Just that fact alone might be enough to put the Raven's life on the line.

No one messed in the affairs of the Wolf.

The Raven was initially surprised at how casual the Wolf had been about the news of the Brotherhood's attack against them at Tocito Wash. And the ultimate loss of his lieutenant, the Vulture, hadn't seemed to faze him at all.

The Brotherhood was strong. The Skinwalkers were all well aware that they were formidable foes.

One of the reasons the Wolf hadn't been more furious over their most recent defeat was that he'd learned the

Vulture had held out against the Brotherhood until death. That fact alone pacified him.

But the information the Raven had just received had put a sharp prickle down his spine. Questions were being raised about his faked research, and he'd sent feelers out to find out who was making the inquiries.

He had originally assumed it would be a scientist from a competing laboratory who was trying to undermine their chances of getting the grant. But a name had just popped up on his computer screen that would likely mean his life could be measured in mere hours from now until his final demise.

Dr. Victoria Sommer. The *bilagáana* woman doctor whom he'd thought he controlled.

She was supposed to be impotent. Out of touch up at Ben Wauneka's remote clinic, and fumbling her way through learning the Navajo language and some alternative cures. Or so he'd assumed.

Apparently he'd been wrong.

The Raven needed more information, and he needed it fast. How had she stumbled across their scam? More importantly, who had she talked to and what had she told them? Just what the hell did she know?

Did she know anything about Skinwalkers? Or was she simply meddling in Navajo affairs because she was a do-gooder, a busybody?

He scrambled back to his computer and tried to think. Who could he call on to get information without the Wolf finding out?

Everything was about to come crashing down around him. Would it all be caused by a blond doctor who didn't recognize her place?

He cursed her with an ancient chant and let his fingers fly across the keyboard. Someone out there in cyberspace had to come to his aid. And they'd better come fast. If the Wolf got wind of this first, it would be all over for both the Raven and the useless Anglo doctor.

She'd been sleeping in his bed for close to a week and Ben had never been so happy. But his gut instinct told him their time together would be measured in days, not weeks or months as he might've preferred.

He sat in the shade on his new swing and watched Tory gliding across the garden. She bent to caress the plants and it reminded him of her patting the faces of both an old woman who was dying all alone and a chubby-cheeked child with poison oak who wasn't sleeping due to the scratching.

The patients seemed to love her. And she loved them in return.

Of course, the plants in his garden loved her, too. They were thriving and strong under her care. She'd learned so much from the Plant Tender.

But no miracle would be able to hold back his disease. He knew the truth now. Days and days had gone by when he saw nothing at all. More and more of those days it seemed than the ones like today, during which he could see a little daylight.

When the end of his sight came for good, he would have to give up his practice entirely. No one came to a crystal gazer who could not see.

At that point, Tory would have to go. But go where? The Brotherhood still had not pinned down the so-called medicine dude from Raven Wash Clinic. So he couldn't let her go back there. It would be too dangerous.

Perhaps he should begin putting out feelers with other small clinics in Dinetah who might be interested in having a good doctor join their staff. The thought made him sigh. He knew it would be tough for any Navajo to accept a blond woman doctor—until they got to know her.

Worse than worrying about where she would go, how could *he* learn to live with solitary nights once again? That might seem a little selfish. But damn it, he couldn't stand the thought of never hearing her laugh, and never again feeling her warm skin as she cuddled up against him in the darkness.

Ben sat for another hour, watching Tory work in the garden. He wanted to soak up enough memories of her to last him for a lifetime. She had on that funny straw hat Shirley had given her and the picture she made was unforgettable.

Finally, the azure sky and the cotton-candy clouds gave way to dusk, which stole across the sky with its streaks of copper and smoke. It was time to go inside for the day. Inside to where the two of them could talk and laugh and be together through the long black of endless night.

"It's getting late," Ben called out. "Time for us to start dinner." He'd come to at least one decision. Tonight was the time to talk to her about his eyesight and how limited the choices would be when he lost it for good.

Tory's head came up and she smiled over at him. "Do you think there might be enough daylight for me to come back out later? I have two more transplants to put in."

"Probably not. Look around. The sunset is settling in over the Chuskas already."

"All right. Since you're still seeing so well this afternoon, why don't you go ahead? I'll just zip in to your office and check my e-mail."

Something about the way she said that last sentence put a dagger of fear down his spine. He wasn't sure what could be so wrong, but he knew the smell of danger and it had suddenly permeated the air around them like a thick fog.

Rising from his chair, Ben stood on the balls of his feet, ready to run. Where was it coming from, this chilling feeling that everything had gone terribly wrong?

"Wait," he said and stopped her before she could enter the office. "Who would be sending you e-mail? Who do you expect to hear from? Your family?"

Her eyebrows raised as though she was surprised he would question her. "Not family, no. I…uh…well, I've been trying to get a line on that phony research lab and I've recently been getting lots of information from my old professor. He's supposed to be sending me a name and perhaps an address. Maybe he already has and it's waiting for me."

She turned to go through the door but he stopped her again by laying a hand on her arm. "I can't believe you did that. I thought we talked about this and decided it would be dangerous for you to keep digging for answers."

"*You* talked. But you didn't say anything I hadn't thought of, so I decided to give it a try. Nothing bad has happened to me."

He heard it then, a shrill cry so high-pitched he almost missed it. When he turned his head to look around, he spotted the coyote standing at the edge of the cedar forest—watching and waiting.

Letting loose a slew of Navajo cuss words, Ben wrapped an arm around Tory's waist and began dragging her toward the house. "Move," he demanded. "Don't run, but walk as fast as you can."

"What on earth is wrong with you? Why?"

"See the coyote over there, Doctor?"

She turned her head, and he heard her short, sharp gasp when she spotted the animal not more than fifty feet away.

"He hasn't come on any damned social call," he grumbled with the irritation plain in his voice. "The coyote is here as a warning. You're in danger." Ben urged her to move faster.

"What do you mean? I don't understand."

"I'll explain it as soon as we're safely inside." He picked up his speed and realized he was carrying her again. "In fact, we'll have a nice long chat—about a lot of things."

He was running now, pushing past the garden plants and heading for the back door. Yeah. No matter what she thought about the things he would tell her, or even what she would think of him, Ben was done keeping her in the dark.

She was going to hear everything. He was the only one who had a good reason to remain blind and in the dark.

Tory was out of breath by the time the back door was safely locked behind them. But when she turned to check on Ben, she found him already on the cell phone to the Brotherhood.

Gritting her teeth, she spun the other way and went into the kitchen to start dinner. Tory loved Ben Wauneka and had enormous respect for him as a doctor and as a much-needed medicine man for his People. But this Brotherhood thing was simply beyond her.

A few minutes later he joined her at the sink. "The Brotherhood will be sending…someone…to stand guard over us tonight. But don't worry, you won't even know they're around. They'll stay outside. I believe we would've been okay in here anyway since the house has had a special Blessing Ceremony. But it's better to be sure we'll be safe."

"Outside? Someone I know will be outside all night?"

Ben shook his head. "Not someone you know."

Sometimes the man said the most intriguing and infuriating things. And always right afterward he would clamp his mouth shut, making it perfectly clear that he would offer no explanation.

Together they fixed themselves a light supper. The bulk of the preparation and eating was done in a tight web of silence.

At last they were back at the sink, washing and drying their few dishes. Tory couldn't stand it anymore.

So many questions were bubbling around in her head. Why was she in such danger? Who would come after her for just asking questions and why was Ben so sure that somebody would? What was it about the coyote that had been so threatening? The wild animal had made no moves to come toward them and had simply stood and watched.

But the first thing that came out of her mouth was the question that had been burning in her brain for weeks now. "Tell me about the Brotherhood," she demanded all of a sudden. "What are their goals and mission? Just who are you guys—really?"

Ben dried the last dish and started a pot of coffee. "Have a seat, Tory. It's a long story, and you're long overdue to hear it."

God, she hoped he wouldn't try to lie to her about anything. So far, some of the things he'd said and some of things they'd been through seemed downright impossible. But she had always been positive he believed every word he'd uttered.

It was all the things he had obviously left out, on purpose, that concerned her.

"Do you remember when I told you there was a long history in Dinetah about the Skinwalkers? You need to hear those legends now." Ben pulled out a chair and sat beside her at the kitchen table.

"I already have. Your great-uncle Hastiin Lakai Begay told me the first part. And Shirley finished the rest of the story off for me one day. But what does any of that have to do with the Brotherhood?"

Ben's face cracked in a wry smile and answered her with a question of his own. "So what did you think about the legend?"

"Shirley seems convinced that there's a real Skinwalker alive and causing trouble on the rez today." She shook her head and looked away from him, not able to meet his gaze. "But it's just so out of the realm of the possible, that I can't accept it."

Ben waited a few beats. "What aren't you saying? I hear the possibilities in your voice."

"It's nothing…" She shook her head again. "Well, some of the things that have happened around us have seemed rather unfathomable, I admit. But still…"

She took a deep breath to get the words out in one fell swoop. "I've been dreaming—a lot—about a creature with yellow eyes and sharp fangs who's chasing us. I know it isn't a coyote or a mountain lion or any other real animal. Somehow, I just know it's a wolf. The Navajo Wolf?"

Ben took her hand with both of his, in a quick protective gesture. "How long have you been dreaming these things? Why didn't you tell me?"

"Tell you what? That a perfectly reasonable medical

professional has nightmares sometimes?" She was already feeling rather foolish just mentioning it now.

He dropped her hand and stood, turning his back to pour the coffee. "Do you trust me?" he asked without looking at her.

"Yes...of course I do." It was one of the few times in their conversation that one of them had simply answered without asking another question of their own.

"Then listen to me with your heart." He brought two mugs of black coffee to the table and sat back down. "Those of us who have been raised with the old Dine traditions know the Skinwalkers well. Too well. We also know that when we mention them to outsiders they will not believe because they have no empirical proof. So we refuse to talk about it.

"For well over fifteen hundred years there has been at least one Navajo Wolf in every generation who has sought to terrorize the Dine," he continued. "More recently, sometime over the last ten years or so, a new Navajo Wolf appeared in a drastically different form from most of them in the generations before him. No one knows who he is or where he came from, but he has organized an army of Navajo compatriots in many freakish personas. They use new communication and technology techniques, along with their superhuman strength, to keep much of Dinetah at their mercy."

Tory was trying not to hyperventilate. But she loved this man with everything she had. If he seriously believed what he was saying, she had to listen—and try to accept it.

"You're having trouble buying the whole idea, I know," he said as if he could read her mind. "But hear me through."

She nodded, but grabbed hold of her coffee mug with both hands. The heat on her fingers and the familiar smell of the liquid caffeine had to be enough to keep her grounded.

"About five years ago," he went on, "Shirley Nez uncovered the truth of the Dine's newest threat. I was the one she contacted first about it. I was in my last year of residency. But I had been spending every free moment back here taking medicine man training with several of our elders and learning plant remedies from Shirley and my great-grandmother."

He stopped to take a breath and then stared down, unseeing, into the still full coffee mug before him. Tory was absolutely positive that telling her this was costing him more than she would ever know.

"Like you, I refused to believe. Until I saw one of them change over with my own eyes. Soon enough I realized the evil was spreading across Dinetah and pushing out past its boundaries. Shirley suggested that a few of us, mostly cousins from my clan, band together to secretly fight them off."

"The Brotherhood," she whispered without thinking.

He shot her a quick look before he went back to studying his coffee mug. "Yes. I'm not sure where or how she uncovered such things. But within a year, Shirley had found some old chants and a couple of sacred medicine man potions that are capable of holding the Skinwalkers at bay so we stand a chance of fighting them off."

"Really? Do they..." She choked on the words. But after swallowing back the disbelief, she tried again. "Do these chants and potions give superhuman strength to the Brotherhood, too?"

Shaking his head, he grimaced but still refused to look

at her. "I agree. It would be great if this were a comic book story. But it isn't, Tory. It's real life. *My* real life."

He sighed. "That cult those teenage athletes found so compelling is really a Skinwalker recruitment ploy. The enemy is using mind control. And a centuries-old white powder we haven't been able to analyze that appears capable of either paralyzing a victim or turning one into a Skinwalker with repeated use."

Dazed at his words, she took a sip of coffee only to realize it had grown cold while he'd told his story.

"Ben. That's…that's incredible. Are you sure that's what's really happening? Don't you think it could possibly be some sort of mass hysteria?"

"I only wish it was. The Brotherhood uncovered the fact that the plant thieves were being led by Skinwalkers. When we went to confront them last week, there was a skirmish between us. Unfortunately…"

"What do you mean? Like a battle? You could've been hurt. Kody Long promised me you'd be okay."

"Shush, tigress," he said and at long last looked at her again. "You see that I'm fine. Shirley's ancient chants keep us safe enough. What I meant in telling you, was to let you know that I myself witnessed Coach Singleton turn himself into a vulture. We had no choice but to…"

Tory waved her hands in front of her face, trying to stave off his words. "I don't want to know."

She laid her head down on the table, trying to absorb— no, truthfully, she was trying to *avoid* thinking about all he'd said. It was too much to even consider.

Ben rose and came to stand beside her. "My eyesight is going out again. Come to bed with me for now. We can finish this discussion later. After you've rested and have had a chance to clear your head."

Absently, Tory nodded. She couldn't think. Could barely move. It felt like some evil spirit had paralyzed her with mind control.

Ben pulled her up from the chair, lifted her into his arms and took them both off to his bedroom.

Through the night, Tory reached for him again and again. At times it was to crush his lips with demanding, hungry kisses. At other times it was to roll into his embrace so he could soothe and rub her back as she whimpered in her sleep.

Ben was lost. Lost in the force of their coming together. Lost in the emotions she had wrung from him. And lost because he knew that much worse things were still left to be said between them.

In the darkest hour of the night, he reached for her. Intending to pull her to him and declare his love, he was surprised to find the bed empty beside him.

"Tory? Tory, where are you?"

Still quite blind, Ben crawled out of bed and felt his way through the familiar house, calling her name. A momentary panic raced through him when she didn't answer. She wouldn't have gone outside, would she?

"Answer me," he demanded.

He heard her shift in the darkness. "Tory?"

Suddenly she was beside him, taking his arm and whispering in his ear. "Why are you up? I'm right here. I would never leave you alone in the dark."

He heard it in her voice just as clearly as if she'd spoken the words aloud. She wouldn't leave him alone, but she would be leaving him soon.

He knew she was right. It had to be that way. But it still hurt.

"I've been sitting on the couch, looking out the window at all the stars," she said in a gentle voice. "Do you want to come sit with me?"

"You know there is more to say."

"Yes, I know." She took his hand.

He sat on the couch and pulled her onto his lap. Sighing, Tory rested her head on his shoulder.

"I've done more than put myself in danger, haven't I?" she asked rhetorically. "I've probably ruined your chances of finding out who's behind the drug cure scam."

"If they're as clever as we think they are, the evil ones are no doubt heading further undercover right this minute. But it doesn't really matter. We'll get them the next time. What matters is that you're okay."

"You're going to ask me to leave. Not just to leave your house, but leave all of Dinetah, aren't you? I truly don't belong here."

"It's for the best."

"But I thought I was…" she hesitated and he wished like hell he could see her expression. "Shirley Nez keeps telling me I'm meant to be her assistant. She says I'm more Navajo in the way I've taken to the Plant Clan than most of the real Dine."

His heart began to weep over its coming loss.

"You're in the ultimate danger in every part of the rez," he told her. "We can't protect you everywhere, all the time. I don't like it, either, but you have to go."

"What about you? Who will take care of you, and your practice?"

"I don't have any time left. Maybe a day or two at most before the disease wins for good. You know it as well as I do."

She put her arms around his neck and buried her face

in his shoulder. "I could do it all. I swear. Except for the crystal gazing. But maybe your patients would…"

He chuckled at her resistance, because he'd thought of all the possibilities himself. "No," he said gently. "I know you would try. But it's better if I just shut down."

"How will you live?"

"I'll be fine. I have several spinster cousins who have volunteered to come live here and be my housekeeper."

"Would you marry one? Like in the old traditions?"

"You don't know everything you think you do." He laughed. "Dine are never allowed to marry another from their 'born to' clan. Further, it is doubtful any woman would want to tie herself to a crystal gazer who has been witched and cannot see."

"I feel like I don't know anything anymore. I don't know where I'll go if I leave the reservation. I still have a contract and I haven't yet paid off my school loan."

Ben buried his nose in her hair to smell the sage one last time. "I'll buy off your contract and pay off your loan. You can go wherever you want. Wherever in the world you feel you're needed."

"You'll pay off my loan? How?"

That made him smile. "You know, for a street-savvy woman, you can be pretty unobservant sometimes. My father set me up with a huge trust fund right after my mother died. That's what pays for everything around here.

"How did you think I was running the clinic?" he added. "Think about it. You've never seen any patient pay, and not once has an insurance or government form been filled out."

"But I thought the Tribal Council supported you."

"The amount they grant wouldn't pay our pharmacy bills for one day per week."

"Oh, sheesh." She gulped. "You're rich."

Yeah, he was rich. Rich in every way it didn't matter. But when she left, he would be the poorest man on earth.

Chapter 17

Heartsick and beyond rattled by everything she'd learned over the last twelve hours, Tory drove down the grade from Ben's mesa. Lucas Tso was in the passenger seat instead of the man she loved, and her brain still spun with thoughts of Skinwalkers. She headed into the bright golden daylight of early morning with a deep black cloud overhanging her heart.

The pink slip for Ben's SUV was now in her suitcase. And the pain of losing him was already wedging itself deep inside her every cell.

Amazing her own city-savvy little self, she really did believe the Skinwalker story. She suspected the legend had always made sense to her Irish soul, but her practical side hadn't wanted to accept it.

She was, after the initial disbelief, truly glad her new Dine friends had such good protection in the form of the

Brotherhood. Not that any of this knowledge would do her much good in New York or California or any other damned place where she might end up.

No, if anything, she would be well advised to wipe all legends and ideas from her brain the minute she crossed the border and left the Navajo Nation. But there were a few things she would never forget. The warm brown eyes of a gentle and very sexy doctor were on the top of that list.

The ache in her chest at the thought of never seeing Ben again, never seeing the cliffs and mountains and colors of Dinetah again, hurt so badly she nearly doubled over the steering wheel. But Lucas's quiet, watchful presence beside her meant she had to keep her eyes on the road ahead and her foot on an accelerator that was taking her farther away from where she wanted to be with every mile.

His job was to guard her until she arrived back at the rental house on Bluebird Ridge. After that, apparently, the Bird People would be keeping an eye on her as she packed and left the rez.

Okay, so the Bird People concept seemed one step too far for her brain to comprehend, even considering her childhood belief in leprechauns. But then, if she could accept that human beings had learned to turn themselves into animals—and ones with superhuman strength at that—then birds who stood guard for their human friends shouldn't be that big a stretch.

In a way, she would've liked to have a long conversation with Lucas Tso. There were questions that remained unanswered. He also seemed like a nice guy who had a tremendous artistic talent and would be an interesting person to talk to.

But every time she went to open her mouth, the tears

welled in her eyes and began to burn in the back of her throat. She never cried.

Tory didn't say anything and within the hour was back at the tiny house with the wonderful garden in back she'd planted months ago. Lucas bid her farewell and soon she was all alone again. She needed to pack, and she wanted a second to say goodbye to her garden plants.

Each dragging step she took, though, made it clear a nap would be a much better idea before she did anything else. Her brain needed to rest. And her body ached almost as badly as her heart from a night filled with both passion and despair.

Going into her bedroom, having to face the bed where she and Ben had first discovered each other, seemed too difficult after everything else. So she collapsed on the sofa and fell into a dreamless sleep. No wolves chased her this time, and no warm brown eyes showed up to caress her with their loving gaze.

"I disagree, Raven," the Navajo Wolf said carefully through the satellite phone. "We can turn the situation around quite quickly if the Anglo woman doctor joins with us, recants her objections and signs on as a researcher with our team. Her change of attitude will seem quite realistic and will add enormously to our veracity with the pharmaceutical company."

"We don't have a team," the Raven managed. "And if we did, I can't see how Dr. Sommer is going to suddenly have such a change of heart."

The low, feral growl from the other end of the phone upped the Raven's panic. He found himself cowering behind his desk, though the Wolf was undoubtedly hundreds of miles away.

"Think of a way—or else, Raven. I suggest kidnapping her and using the powder to make her see the light. She's left the protection of the Brotherhood now. It should be easy to get her alone and spirit her away. No one will notice…or care."

"But…"

"Just do it," the Wolf insisted. "And then contact me with good news for a change. I'll expect to hear from you soon that all is in order."

When Tory woke up groggy and irritable, she decided to put off packing until she went to the Raven Wash Clinic to tell Dr. Hardeen goodbye. She would never leave the reservation without explaining to him about Ben paying off her contract and loan. Ray Hardeen had been a good boss and had treated her with respect, even though many of his patients hadn't wanted anything to do with her.

Splashing water on her face, she decided that she owed a great deal to Dr. Hardeen. This would be an opportunity to tell him thanks.

Twenty minutes later, she drove into the Raven Wash Clinic's parking lot. Heaving a sigh of both relief and misery, she was glad to see that Dr. Hardeen's car was there. Saying goodbye was going to be difficult.

After knocking on his door and hearing nothing, she peeked inside. His back was to her as he stared at his computer screen.

"Dr. Hardeen?"

He turned, and it was everything Tory could do to keep her gasp of surprise hidden. The man seemed to have aged twenty years in the last few weeks. His hair was much grayer, his eyes droopy, and his facial skin was wrinkled and cracked as though he'd spent the last three weeks in the sun.

"Dr. Sommer? Tory. Come in. What can I do for you?"

She wondered if there was something she could do for him. But she didn't say anything. Instead she told him she was leaving and that Ben would be paying off her loan.

"Are you sure I can't say anything to change your mind?"

She shook her head. "No. But thanks for asking."

"Well, there is one more thing," he began.

It was then she noticed something strange in his eyes. Fear. Panic. The man sitting in front of her was petrified of something.

"I'll need to check the rental house on Bluebird Ridge and get the keys from you," he continued. "That shouldn't be a problem, right? Would later this afternoon be okay?"

"Uh, sure. No problem. Just as long as I have a couple of hours of daylight left to get on the road."

"Good. Good," he said absently. Obviously, she was being dismissed. "See you later."

She wanted to talk. Find out what was bothering him. Did he know about the Skinwalkers? She would bet he did.

"Um, Dr. Hardeen, can I ask you…?"

"Later, Tory," he interrupted. "We'll talk then."

As she left his office, the creepy feeling that something was terribly wrong with Dr. Hardeen—and maybe with the entire Raven Wash Clinic—engulfed her and left her shaken. She picked up her speed, wanting to reach the sunlight and the safety of Ben's SUV. Well, *her* SUV now.

But as she was almost to the outside door, someone grabbed her from behind. The air whooshed from her lungs.

"Dr. Sommer, wait." Russel, the nurse-practitioner, spun her around.

"You'll be happy to know I'm leaving Dinetah forever," she spat out, trying to wrench her arm from his grip.

His expression looked nearly as spooked as Dr. Hardeen's. "That will be good for you but not good for the Dine, Doctor." His eyes narrowed, boring into hers. "But you've just made a terrible mistake. Coming here was extremely foolhardy. Get in your car and leave the rez now. Do not stop or look back. Your life hangs in the balance."

A threat? She planted her feet and popped her arm free. "I'm leaving." Spinning away from him, she ran the rest of the way to the parking lot.

Was it possible Russel was a Skinwalker? The medicine dude? God, she couldn't get out of this place fast enough.

Breathing hard, she jumped in the SUV, locked the door and dug out the cell phone she'd forgotten to give back.

Shirley Nez punched the off button on her cell phone and basked in sunshine, while the shadow of death slowly moved to cover her spirit. She had been the Brotherhood member to get Tory's call for a reason. The *Yei* were already at work to make her visions a reality.

There were one or two more things left for her to do. But then, she would meet with the new Plant Tender and give her the last lesson. Perhaps, for her and for the Brotherhood, the most important of all the lessons.

Everything was turning out as foreseen. Shirley picked up her phone and began making the calls that would mean new hope for the Dine—and perhaps for the entire world.

"Do you know why the Plant Tender requires our presence today?" Lucas Tso had been the last to arrive at the ancient and seldom used medicine man gathering place atop Bluebird Ridge Mesa.

Ben shrugged. "No, cousin. But I'm grateful to see some of the sights of our sacred land again. There is not much time left for me to see anything. And I'd hate to forever miss the beauty of this place used by our elders."

Today might be the very last day he would have an opportunity to memorize the sights of his beloved land. A fuzzy haze had once more replaced the blackness for a few hours, but his gut told him that it wouldn't last long.

He stood at the edge of the cliff and gazed down into the backyard of Tory's rental house. His heart turned over at the vague image of his SUV parked in front. She must still be packing. Would the *Yei* smile on him yet another time? Might Tory step outside to her garden before leaving?

It would be difficult standing where he could actually see her, but not be with her. Yet one more chance to see her lovely hair and feel her warmth, even from this distance, would be the greatest of blessings.

"You still believe it's for the best to send her away?" Kody Long had quietly come up behind him.

"It is the best for her."

Kody screwed up his face as though he'd tasted something sour. "It's *you* that doesn't want her here. First off, you don't want to be dependent on her in your blindness. You couldn't stand not being the strong one. And secondly, you have some strange notion your mother would only have wanted a Navajo woman for you. But you don't know that for sure."

"Hey," Ben grumbled. "Leave my mother out of it."

"And don't give me that crap about tradition, either," Kody argued. "You know I don't buy it. My wife's presence hasn't caused anything to be out of balance or in chaos. In fact, she's been really useful to the Brotherhood when it comes to fighting the Skinwalkers by getting information A little while ago Reagan even pinned down the name of the 'medicine dude' at Raven Wash Clinic."

"Really? Who is it?"

"I'm waiting for Shirley Nez to show up to tell everyone at one time. Then we can make plans to take him out or at least neutralize his efforts."

"I think you may have a longer wait, cousin," Lucas said. He stood next to Ben and pointed down toward where Shirley's old pickup was pulling into Tory's yard.

"What the hell is the Plant Tender doing down there?" Kody threw his hands up. "She's already late to meet us."

Ben didn't like the odd feeling that was creeping into his bones. Something about this whole setup seemed wrong.

"Lucas, are you experiencing something strange?" he asked his sensitive cousin.

"I feel we are needed elsewhere." He pointed again as Shirley tore out of her truck and dashed into the house. "The Plant Tender needs our help down there."

"Uh-oh," Kody muttered. "Look. See that shiny black limo just heading around the farthest bend in Bluebird Road? That thing seems dangerous. Out of place."

"I recently heard that Dr. Ray Hardeen of Raven Wash Clinic has purchased such a vehicle," Lucas told them.

Ben grabbed Kody's arm. "Tell me the *medicine dude* Reagan uncovered isn't Hardeen."

Kody grimaced. "Let's move out. He'll be there in less than five minutes. All of us need to begin the special chanting—now."

"I didn't expect to see you here, Plant Tender." Tory stood aside and invited Shirley Nez to step inside the air-conditioned rental house. "Did you reach the Brother-hood to tell them Russel Beyal is probably the medicine dude they've been looking for?"

"There isn't much time," Shirley said quietly, without answering her question. "I have something to tell you."

"Okay." Tory wondered why her friend was being so obtuse and weirded out. "You want something cool to drink? I'm done packing and was just about to haul the suitcases out to the SUV, but I can take a moment to sit down and have a glass of iced tea with you."

Shirley turned her head and stared out the front window. "No drink, thanks. Let's go out to the garden. There is one more important plant remedy I must explain. We'll have an extra minute or two alone out back."

Another plant remedy? But Tory was leaving the res-ervation for good. What possible use would it be for her to know about another plant at this stage?

Something appeared to be terribly wrong with Shirley Nez today. But the Plant Tender had been so good to her over the last few weeks. So good *for* her, becoming a friend when everyone else seemed to hate her for being white.

Tory shrugged a shoulder and let Shirley lead them out the back door and into her garden. The least she could do in repayment for all her kindness was to humor the woman and spend a final few minutes with her.

"It's the skunk-smelling raggedy goat sage," Shirley said on a shaky breath when they'd stopped at the far edge of the garden.

"Excuse me?"

"Hastiin Lakai Begay's reminder. It finally hit me what he meant." Shirley grabbed her hand and squeezed. "It's the cure for Ben Wauneka's blindness."

"What?" The breath left Tory's lungs and her knees grew weak and trembling. "Are you sure? Calm down and tell me everything. How can it help and what do you do with it? Is the remedy a drink? Where can the plant be found?"

Shirley was shaking her head. "No time. Just listen. It should be made into a vinegar tincture, not the usual tea remedy. Apply it to both sides of the face, to both temples and each eyelid. Ask Michael Ayze to sing the necessary chant. It's old, nearly forgotten. But he will remember."

Tory's head was swirling. Hopes. Dreams. Entire futures were suddenly looming before her.

She heard brakes squealing in her front yard. Who? Oh, yes. It was probably Dr. Hardeen coming to pick up the keys. But there were so many more questions she had to ask.

"Plant Tender, quick, I have guests coming. Tell me where this Plant Clan can be found."

She looked over to Shirley just as the woman's face paled. What on earth was the matter with her? Please don't be having a heart attack or a stroke, Tory begged her silently. Not now.

"Why did you tell *me?*" Tory demanded. "Why not Ben?"

"You are the tender of the Plant Clan from now on," Shirley replied in a whisper. "It will be your job to keep the knowledge and to pass on the information. But this Plant Clan is hidden and will be hard to see."

Tory could hear someone knocking on her front door with persistence. But her brain was trying to absorb what Shirley was saying.

"Me, a Plant Tender? But, I'm leaving Dinetah. Besides, you're the Plant Tender."

Reaching up to tenderly cup Tory's cheek, Shirley Nez

shook her head. "Remember well the principles I've taught you. We didn't have enough time, but I will be leaving you with the *knowledge.* You are destined to be one of the best Plant Tenders in all Dine history."

The knocking had stopped. Tory was worried that Dr. Hardeen would leave and then she would have to search him out to turn over the keys. But her friend Shirley sounded crazy. Could she be having some kind of attack, or be about to go into a diabetic coma?

"Just hold on a second, Plant Tender," she said gently. "Come inside where it's cooler and let me answer the door. If you can wait a few minutes, we'll finish this discussion. You have me confused."

Tory turned but Shirley pulled her back. "The danger is already here, new Plant Tender. It walks on two feet but don't let that fool you."

"Tory! Oh, there you are," a male voice called out to her. She turned to find Dr. Hardeen waving as he and a couple of other men came walking around the side of the house.

"Run." Shirley pushed at her back. "Run. Hide in the junipers and piñons. Help is on the way."

Run? "But what's wrong?"

"Go now." Shirley put herself between Tory and the men, closed her eyes and began to sing a chant.

Tory looked past Shirley to Dr. Hardeen. The man she saw coming toward her through the garden was not the man she thought she knew. The face was the same, or almost the same, with the addition of many wrinkles and odd scarring.

But the eyes were entirely different. Black and beady, they were not the eyes of the kind doctor who'd been her boss—or even of the dangerous wolf in her dreams. But they did remind her of something. Something terrifying.

Fear snaked through her. She backed up a couple of steps. *Run.* Petrified, she didn't want to stay where she was, but she couldn't leave her friend, either.

"Come on now, Tory," Dr. Hardeen, or whoever it was, called to her. "I just want to talk. I have a fabulous new proposition for you."

"Begone!" Shirley admonished him in Navajo. "You may *not* have her. The forces of good forbid it."

"Be gone yourself, Plant Tender," he said with a flourish of his hand. "The *bilagáana* woman has meddled into things that do not concern her and she will be given an opportunity to make that right."

Tory's feet were itching to turn and run. She backed up a few more steps, putting another five or six feet between them. But she still could not bear to leave Shirley alone to face whatever evil this was.

"Ah," Shirley said with a half laugh. "I see you believe your minutes on earth are also numbered. But it's too easy for you to die quickly, Skinwalker. You deserve pain. You deserve to face the anger of your master. Too bad you will not have the chance.

"As a doctor, you could've done much good for the People," she added. "But you chose the dark wind instead."

"Shut up, woman. It's not my pain that should concern you. Get out of the way."

Tory was horrified when she noticed that the hands of both men who'd come with Dr. Hardeen had become claws. What should've been fingers were flexing sharp, hooked nails under the cuffs of long-sleeved shirts. *Ohmigod.* This was no hallucination.

She looked around for some kind of weapon. But what did someone use against an evil demon?

Taking two more steps backward in the direction of the

dense juniper bushes, Tory spotted a large, heavy-looking rock. If only she could get to it without them noticing, then maybe she could help Shirley.

"Dr. Sommer," the evil one with Dr. Hardeen's face said through gritted teeth. "You have one minute to come with us of your own free will. After that, I cannot be responsible for what happens."

The noise came first from directly above her head. The sound was sharp, high-pitched. She glanced up, afraid to take her eyes off Dr. Hardeen for long.

Birds were circling the area. Big birds for the most part. Hawks, eagles. So many she couldn't be sure of all the species.

The icy fingers of truth reached out and grabbed her by the throat. The raven. That was where she'd seen those eyes in Dr. Hardeen's face before.

The evil doctor cursed them all in Navajo. Before her very eyes, the images of the two men with him blurred and became indistinct for a few seconds. Tory blinked and when she looked again, the two men had become huge vultures. They spread their large, vicious wings and flew up to do battle in the sky with the hawks and eagles.

Tory reached down and palmed the rock while everyone's attentions were turned to the skies above. A gun might've been better protection. But on the other hand, she wouldn't have the foggiest idea of how to use one.

That thought gave her a momentary pause. When the time came, would she be able to use the rock? Could she manage to hit another human being with murderous intent? That was *not* who she was.

"Get out of my way," Dr. Hardeen screamed at Shirley. "It's over. I will win."

Shirley shook her head and stood her ground.

.

Just then new sounds could be heard in the distance, this time coming from the road in front of the house. Trucks, SUVs. A group of vehicles was arriving, streaking into her yard.

More bad guys? If so, Tory figured she had waited too long to run. All was lost.

The clearest voice she could recognize belonged to Ben, as he called her name. The good guys to the rescue.

Tory took her first real breath in what seemed like a half hour. She turned her face toward the voice of the man she loved, just the same as Shirley Nez had turned to see the Brotherhood rushing for them. A whole army of men came racing around the side of the house.

But their loss of focus came at the worst possible moment. Tory heard a high-pitched shriek that sounded more like anger than anything else, and she turned back to stare at the evil dressed in her boss's body.

He shrieked again, cursing and squawking as he shook a bony fist at them. Then he turned into a bird right in front of her eyes. Black. Dangerous. The raven.

She cowered, momentarily stung by the impossibility of what she had seen. In the time it took her to grit her teeth and stand tall to face the evil, the raven had spread its wings and was diving straight for her.

Shirley Nez stepped in front of the attacker. *No!*

So angry she could barely see, Tory hefted the rock and ran to save her friend. Blinded by revulsion and furious at the senseless invasion, she waded into a whirlwind of feathers and claws, swinging the rock over her head with as much force as she could muster.

No. No. No. Damn it. If she was destined to die today, this unholy bird was—by all the saints—going to go with her.

Chapter 18

"I can't believe she's dead. It doesn't seem possible."

In his mind's eye, Ben could see Tory shaking her head as she drove him up the ridge toward Shirley Nez's house. The funeral and memorial were already over. In the Navajo tradition, the Plant Tender's earthly body had been buried as soon as could be arranged. The sunrise memorial over her gravesite had been both beautiful for him to hear and gut-wrenching for everyone in attendance.

But Ben couldn't help wondering where the Plant Tender's spirit would be residing. The best of Shirley Nez was nearby. He could feel her presence in the air around them. He'd known her well, knew she would never leave the Brotherhood alone without her spirit, not while the Skinwalker war persisted.

Sixteen hours after the battle with the Skinwalkers had gone by, though, and Ben realized his beloved Tory was still blaming herself for the Plant Tender's death. The beautiful Anglo doctor was also having trouble adapting to reality.

Accepting that she might not be the same healer she had always imagined herself to be must be a difficult challenge. Somehow, even with all her physician's "do no harm" instincts, she'd nevertheless contributed to the death of Dr. Hardeen in his raven persona. And with a baseball-size rock, no less.

Ben had tried to explain that chances were good the raven's death was caused more by the Brotherhood's chanting, along with assistance from Hunter Long's knife, than by anything she'd done. Still, at least one of her blows had connected and that was enough to convince Tory she had ended the existence of the Skinwalker.

The thought of her wading into the battle actually made him smile, right through the continuing pain of losing his mentor. Tory couldn't stop herself from being a protector. A mother tigress.

But he wasn't sure what to say now to help her through the pain and guilt. He was still sure she was in mortal danger and should be leaving the rez as fast as possible. That was all he could think of. A raven might be dead, but the Navajo Wolf still controlled evil across Dinetah.

"The Plant Tender's death seems senseless," he finally muttered. "If I didn't know better, I would say she deliberately put herself in harm's way. The Plant Tender should've asked the Brotherhood to plan an ambush if she somehow knew you would be attacked." Though Ben *did* admit he would never have allowed anyone to use Tory as bait. Not even Shirley Nez.

"I think she wanted me to see…really see for myself…what the Dine are up against," Tory said softly. "I know it's made a big difference in how I think.

"And the Plant Tender also seemed quite determined to make me accept that there is a cure to be found for your eye disease," Tory added.

"I'm not as sure about that part as you seem to be," Ben grumbled from behind his blank, unseeing eyes. "I've never even heard of skunk-smelling raggedy goat sage. My great-grandmother was the Plant Tender before Shirley Nez, and as a kid I talked to hundreds of elders and old medicine men about cures. Why don't I know that one?"

"I've told you," Tory argued. "Hastiin Lakai Begay had to remind even Shirley Nez about that particular Plant Clan. And then she mentioned to me it had all but disappeared and would be hard to locate."

Ben refused to let the worm of hope crawl inside his defenses. His Anglo physician's training warred with every Navajo belief. There was no cure for his disease.

And even if this Plant Clan did exist somewhere in Navajoland, now that Shirley was gone they would never find it. So he stopped thinking about cures. Stopped wondering what if.

"You're sure no one will mind if I stay at Shirley's house—at least temporarily?"

Tory was deliberately changing the subject for now and that was fine by him. "No Navajo would want to be inside that house for a while, and you will be safe there until you feel ready to leave the rez. There is no way for you to be comfortable now in the place on Bluebird Ridge. And more, I would be concerned with your safety.

"The Plant Tender is—was—a neighbor to Kody and Reagan," he added. "So you won't be too far from help. And Shirley's house has been specially blessed and protected."

Her silence told him something he had said was bothering her. But Ben wasn't sure if it was the fact that he hadn't invited her to come up to his house that upset Tory. Or if she was uncomfortable with Kody and Reagan, people she barely knew.

"I really liked Reagan Long when I met her this morning. She's cool. How long have they been married?"

That response pretty much said everything. But Ben refused to be sorry he had not invited Tory to come back to his house. Tonight his cousin Issy Whitehorse would be coming to take care of him, and Ben had already settled his mind to never having Tory in his home again. To never being able to see her sweet image again. The blindness had closed in on him for good.

He couldn't bear having to go through the pain of getting Tory back in his bed and in his arms, when he would only have to send her away once more. Stiffening his spine to the inevitable, Ben tried to continue the small talk.

"The Longs have been married since the first of the year. They're newlyweds." His voice sounded a lot steadier than he felt.

"Hmm. That's nice. They're a nice couple."

Hmm, was right. Something far different than living arrangements seemed to be bothering her. Ben waited for Tory to tell him what it was.

"What's going to happen to Raven Wash Clinic now that…well, now that the director is gone?"

Ben wasn't sure why, but he didn't think this question would lead to the root of her problem, either.

He silently agreed to talk on whatever subject she wanted. "As soon as I get you settled, Hunter Long will be picking me up. Raven Wash Clinic is our first stop. I intend to do everything in my power to see that it remains open. It provides a much-needed service to the Dine."

"Funny," she said, but there was no humor in her voice. "Dr. Hardeen said those exact words about your clinic."

"Tory…there is no such thing as all good or all evil. It would be wonderful if we could simply diagnose the dark wind in people and then cut it out like a cancer. But we can't—at least not yet. Ray Hardeen chose his path. He took the wrong fork and opted for greed. No one else could've stopped it nor prevented it. He sealed his own fate."

She sighed, and he wished like hell he could take her in an embrace and make all the bad images go away. His arms ached to hold her. His heart cracked knowing he could never be there for her again.

"I worry about you going to Raven Wash," she said in a slight change of subject he welcomed. "I think there still might be evil lurking there. You will be careful, won't you? Will Officer Long be in his tribal police uniform, or will he be acting as a member of the Brotherhood?"

"We are always acting as members of the Brotherhood. In everything else we do, that is our first duty."

"Well, there's a nurse-practitioner at the clinic I think you should be careful to avoid. His name is Russel Beyal. Strange guy. I just bet he's a Skinwalker."

Ben felt the smile grow across his face. "You would lose that bet, Doctor. Russel Beyal has been spending all his free hours learning medicine man chants and potions. He was recently apprenticed to an uncle of Lucas Tso, and we expect him to someday become a member of the Brotherhood."

"What? But…" Tory took a breath. "But my friend April Henry hinted that Russel was not what he seemed."

"April Henry was being deluded about a lot of things by her so-called boyfriend, Coach Singleton," Ben told

Tory with great sadness. "We will be working with her to be sure she is fully back in the arms of our clan and breathing in only good spirits instead of the bad."

"Oh." The word had been said in a small voice, not like the woman he loved.

Another long silence from Tory told him that the nut of her biggest concern had not yet been cracked. But instead of telling him what was on her mind, her only words from then on were about directions to Shirley's house.

Perhaps it was just as well. He did not want to know any more of what was in her heart. His own heart had enough problems to fill up the rest of his lonely life—leaving him with nothing but abject misery for company.

Tory breathed deep, and the pungent odor of earth and living things made her feel alive again. When she and Ben had first opened the door to Shirley's double-wide mobile home, it had been such a joyful revelation. Plants. Plants growing everywhere. On nearly every surface.

At first it seemed odd, sad, difficult to be in the Plant Tender's house without her there. But by the time Ben had directed her around with his words instead of his eyes, Tory started feeling right at home.

Ben apparently couldn't wait to get away from there because he'd called Hunter to come pick him up almost as soon as they'd walked in the door. She knew how he felt. It was too difficult for them to remain this close.

Last night…after the battle, several of the participants had had wounds to be tended. Her own small nicks and scrapes were minor and she'd pitched in to suture others and apply the right plant remedies.

But when it came to her injuries, Ben had refused to

let anyone else touch her. Having him salve and bind her wounds caused her much more pain than the actual cuts had done. It took a lot out of her to be that close, to hear him breathing, to feel his heart beating so near to her own.

But on a practical note, no one had needed a hospital. No one had wanted to call the tribal police, either. The Brotherhood took care of each other, buried their enemies and then buried their own.

Tory assumed someone in the Brotherhood would have a way to let outsiders know of the demise of Dr. Hardeen, without actually having to explain the cause. There seemed to be a member of the Brotherhood involved in every aspect of Navajo life.

After Ben had gone away with Hunter, leaving her alone at the Plant Tender's house, Tory thought about all that had taken place. She'd been wrong about so many things.

Perhaps she would even someday apologize to Russel for misjudging his intentions. As she thought back on it now, he had clearly tried to warn her of the danger.

She'd also been wrong to think she could ever walk away from the Dine. Shirley had tried to make it clear, to let her see the duty she had yet to fulfill. It had taken the Plant Tender's death to make Tory a real believer.

So she would be staying for good. Perhaps right here, living in the old Plant Tender's house. And she would learn new remedies, assist the *hataaliis,* and maybe practice a little Anglo medicine from time to time when it was appropriate. She would become the new spinster Plant Tender, living alone and working for the good of the Dine.

Ben still thought she was leaving, and she'd decided the time was not right to tell him any different. But it made her angry that he thought so little of her.

There would be no way for him to guess she had already decided to stay on the rez—no matter what else happened. It wasn't something she wanted to discuss with him yet, either. He wouldn't understand her reasons and would be concerned about her welfare. Not to mention she couldn't bear to hear him tell her once again there was no chance for their future together.

But how could he imagine she would leave when there was any chance at all of helping him to see again?

She went down the hall and opened a side door, thinking it might be the bathroom. Instead she found a room full of files and papers, which was strange for a traditional Navajo home. The Navajo language had only recently been written down and few books had so far been published. Yet stacks of books lined the walls, and there were sticky notes on every other surface.

One clean surface remained on the desk. And right in the middle was a huge manila envelope addressed to her.

Tory plopped down in the swivel chair and gingerly picked up the envelope. She could feel Shirley's presence, not only remaining on the envelope, but everywhere around her. A sheen of wetness blurred Tory's eyes, but she fought it off. No sense crying when there was work to be done. Or some message Shirley Nez had been trying to send.

Spilling the contents of the envelope out onto the desk, Tory was most surprised to find a smaller envelope with Ben's name on it in a writing very different from Shirley Nez's. She set that aside and opened a sheet of paper that had her own name written on the back.

Dear new Plant Tender: If you are reading this it is because my earthly body has gone on to be with the

Yei. I'm sorry to leave you before your training was completed. But continue your learning without me. I bequeath to your care this house, all maps and all lists of remedies within.

Plant Tenders traditionally do not require books or maps to know the cures. But you will be different. You have begun differently, yet I have seen that you will be the greatest Plant Tender of all time. My spirit remains nearby to help you find your way.

Please look at the two small maps I am including in this envelope. I didn't have the time to search, but I believe these to be the best places of finding the skunk-smelling raggedy goat sage. Use your senses to locate it. The name has meaning.

The envelope enclosed with Ben Wauneka's name on it is a letter from his mother. She was my best friend and gave me this for safekeeping right before she died. Her instructions were to give it to him "after his period of blindness and while he was still keeping the blindfold around his heart." I never knew what she'd meant by that strange statement until the doctor fell ill and began fighting his better judgment.

I entrust you now with the fulfillment of my duty. Let your heart tell you when the time is right.

The soft sob escaped Tory's lips before she could call it back. Her new responsibility, the old familiarity of lonely duty. All of that conspired to break her down. But she never cried.

So she sniffed back dry tears and set about studying the maps Shirley had left. Somewhere in Dinetah grew the cure for Ben's blindness. At least, the thing that would make him see again. The blindfold on his heart was another matter entirely, and not in her power to cure.

Ben sat uneasily in the swing, listening to the sound of a truck engine as it labored up the grade toward his home. It was a hot summer afternoon and he had nothing to do but sit in the shade and listen to the birds as cousin Issy, overweight but affable, worked in his garden.

He had shut down his practice for good, but couldn't bear to ignore the garden. The garden Tory had so loved.

In a way, he hated sitting in this swing. Hated the memories of a special dawn when all his problems could be solved by the passionate touches of the woman who'd meant so much. But then again, being here put him nearer to the earth and the plants, reminding him only of the goodness.

He hadn't spoken to Tory in a couple of days. He'd received word that she was fine. Though she didn't appear to be making progress toward leaving the reservation, and it made him wonder what she was waiting for.

Listening to Issy pull weeds and water, Ben let his mind drift away to happier days. Soft breezes sighed through the trees. The smell of cedar and the sounds of the Bird Clan circling overhead conspired to make him miserable. He should never have let Tory get under his skin like this.

Being completely blind was bad enough. Being alone now was a much more horrible fate. He had too much time on his hands to think of how close to losing her life she'd been that afternoon with the Raven.

The truck, not one he recognized but also not one he thought of as dangerous, pulled in front of the house and the engine was turned off. As prescribed by Dine tradition, the driver did not immediately get out but waited a decent interval to be acknowledged.

"Issy, please wave in our visitor. I'm willing to have company." And he would thank the *Yei* for giving him something else to do but feel sorry for himself.

"It is our cousin, Michael Ayze, born to the Big Medicine People, for the Salt Clan," Issy informed him. "He is alone. I'll bring him to you."

After all the usual Navajo greetings, Michael got right to the point. "Everything is ready for your curing sing, cousin. I'll drive you to the ceremony after we visit my sweat hogan first. Your days of darkness are at an end."

"What?" Almost nothing his cousin had said was making any sense—except— "What cure are you talking about?"

"The new Plant Tender has uncovered the skunk-smelling raggedy goat sage. She is preparing it as she was instructed." Michael's tone stopped being so formal and took on a conspiratorial note. "Come on, cuz. You really don't have much choice. No one is willing to say no to your woman when she makes up her mind. Now take my arm. You're supposed to be getting ready. So we're outta here."

An hour or so later, Ben sat alone in the sweat hogan and…well…*sweated* was a good word for it. Willing or not, Michael had dragged him into the pickup, and then a short while later shoved him into the hogan designed specifically to help prepare for ceremonial sings. The smells of sacred plants put into the smoldering fire and the hissing sounds of water on hot coals seemed hypnotic.

Several things Michael said had been rumbling through Ben's mind and now were screaming at him to listen. *The new Plant Tender. Your woman.* What the hell did that mean?

"Open your heart, Ben Wauneka. Open your heart before you open your eyes."

"Shirley Nez?" He recognized the voice but it was impossible. Or…maybe not.

"You are the heart of the Brotherhood," her spirit told him out of his darkness. "Yet you continue to keep your own in a shell. *She* is more a part of the Dine today than you are. But what is it *you* most desire?"

That question took him back. Ben had no answer, but thought he should. Obviously, he wanted to see again. But see what? And more importantly, why?

Twenty hours after they had begun the ceremony, Tory watched as Michael Ayze finally washed the curing potion off of Ben's eyelids and temples. This was the moment of truth.

The other members of the Brotherhood were staying back, out by the bonfire with the rest of the clan members who'd come to the curing ceremony. They had all participated in some way over the course of the long day. And she knew all of them were holding their breaths, waiting for the good result their traditions told them to expect.

She was having a bit more trouble being so positive that the cure would work. But Tory did have the letter from Ben's mother safely tucked into her pocket. That must count for something. She had to believe the news would be good or she wouldn't have brought along something he would have to use his eyes to read. Right?

"Okay, Wauneka," Michael said quietly. "This is it. Open your eyes and tell me what you see."

Watching while Ben worked his granite jaw and blinked, Tory bounced on the balls of her feet and let the tension rule. There was still daylight left; mostly it was just the crimson-and-gold rays of waning sun filling the sky with a rosy hue. But if he could see anything…

Suddenly panic struck, not knowing what he would

want as his first sight, Tory turned her back and held her breath. Afraid to run. Afraid not to.

Slowly, too slowly in Ben's opinion, the yellow haze that had replaced the blackness began to be replaced itself by objects, images. People.

"Tory?" The first clear thing he saw was her cornsilk hair. It was still one of the top two sights in the world as far as he was concerned. But the other one was much more important to him at the moment.

"Tory," he whispered, praying she would turn around.

She did, again too slowly for him. But she could barely manage to make eye contact. And he willed her to.

If you care about me at all, my love, turn those gorgeous blue-grays my way and look at me now.

Lifting her eyelids, she gazed at him with an expression like he had never seen before. It knocked him to his knees and filled his newly clear eyes with tears. He choked back a sob, reached out for her.

She rushed into his arms, fell to her own knees and plastered his face with kisses. "You can see. Oh, thank God. It's worked. Are you okay?"

He gathered her to him, putting every sense to work in the awareness of holding her close. The sweet scent. The silken feel of hair against his neck. The sound of raspy breathing and the soft moans in the back of her throat.

But nothing compared to the moment when he lifted her chin and gazed into her eyes. Just to see those beautiful eyes glowing with love and spilling over with tears.

Reaching out, he used the pad of his thumb to brush back the tears. "I love you so much," he managed to say through a rasp of his own. "And yes, I can see. But I don't want to see anything if it doesn't include you.

"We fit, my love," he added. "I see *that* clearly now.

And I swear on my clan that I will never be far out of sight of you again. Blind or clear. Stay in Dinetah or go. Only please let me be beside you. Now. Forever."

Overcome with the spent tension and breathless emotion, Tory nodded. His mouth covered hers, settled, while their lips melded together in the way their lives always would.

In the back of her mind, she was amazed at all her tears. Tears of relief. Tears of joy. Tears full of the promise of being one with the only man she would ever love.

She had a gut feeling that the Dine's new Plant Tender was going to become a weeper. Soggy, but worth it.

Looking up into the warm brown eyes she so loved, Tory decided yes. Yes, her life from now on was definitely going to be worth every watery drop.